EXILE'S ADORED

ALIEN MATES: PLANET EXILE

KATE RUDOLPH

ABOUT EXILE'S ADORED

Help isn't coming.

When Carise wakes up on an alien planet running is her only chance at escape, even if being caught means death.

She'd rather die than face whatever her captors plan to do to her.

Guerran is no safe place for healing and every moment is fear. Until Jaek, a gentle giant of an alien, makes himself her protector. But when their fragile bond is tested, Carise knows she must find strength within herself to become brave enough to survive Guerran.

This time she won't let herself be taken. And she's not leaving her mate behind.

PROLOGUE

SEVEN YEARS AGO

Jaek ran for all he was worth, each step putting him further away from the market and the scene of his crime. He just had to make it past the walled gardens and into the village yard and the guards would give up.

They always had before.

Ishyr's stomach had rumbled all night, and the boy had choked back any tears his hunger brought on. But he was a child and he couldn't completely hide his pain. And he shouldn't have needed to.

Jaek didn't have coin for bread, but he was big and faster than he looked.

Unfortunately, his height also marked him out. The guards knew to look for him by now, and they'd been ready the second his hands closed over the loaf of stale bread. The cry had gone up and instinct had him running before he realized they were yelling at him.

Jaek's heart beat madly and he couldn't catch a full breath. Dots danced in front of his eyes, and if it weren't for the energy of Krudare that flowed through everyone all the time, he would have already fainted.

He had to make it to the village. The guards *had* to give up.

A uniformed figure stepped in front of him and Jaek skidded to a stop, almost dropping the bread he'd stolen. Jaek looked desperately for a way around the guard, but the man was big and blocking his path. The street narrowed right here and if he turned to go backwards, he'd run into the guards who'd been chasing him.

He was trapped.

"Hand it over," the guard demanded. He clutched a cudgel and patted the blunt end against his hand, a not-so-subtle threat. "Come on, boy, give it up. You've been caught."

Jaek's shoulders slumped. If he didn't get home, the kids would go hungry for another night. Or one of them would try and steal. That was Jaek's job. He took the risks so his young friends didn't have to. They'd all banded together. The streets were hard on orphans, especially the young ones.

Jaek was twenty now, he was old enough to keep them safe.

And old enough for the guards of Krudare to see him as a threat. This wasn't his first time being caught.

If they dragged him before a magistrate, he'd be exiled.

The kids could die. They would have to fend for themselves.

Jaek couldn't let that happen.

With the memory of Ishyr's hunger pangs ringing in his head, Jaek took a deep breath and centered himself. He had to escape. He had to get back.

"There now," said the guard. "Come with me."

Jaek charged. The guard wasn't expecting it, and he grunted as Jaek impacted with him, taking them both to the ground. Jaek might have been young, but he was big, even for a Kru'dari. He had several inches on the guard and he'd been growing muscles faster than he could alter his clothes to fit his new bulk.

He was big, but the guard was skilled. He elbowed Jaek and kicked, sending him flying back. Jaek was lucky to roll out of it and spring back to his feet. He'd assaulted a guard. There was no getting around that. If he didn't get away, they'd exile him for sure.

They clashed again and Jaek let his worries fall to the side. A strange sense of calm washed over him as he fell into the violence of the encounter. Blood bloomed on the guard's face, and it was almost a shock that Jaek's fists had caused it.

Another punch had the guard slumping over unconscious.

That had been almost easy.

Jaek wanted to throw up.

He bent to pick up the fallen bread. He had to get

away before the guard woke up. If he could run fast enough, maybe they wouldn't find him.

But they'd be looking for him.

He had to leave the city.

Thoughts whirred through his head, but Jaek couldn't get caught up in them. The bread was a bit squished, but that didn't matter. The kids would eat tonight.

He turned to head toward the village, and that was his undoing. He heard a yell of warning before bright light flashed and a shot of blaster fire hit him square in the back.

He was unconscious before he hit the ground.

1

Carise Fletcher woke up.

Unfortunately.

She didn't move. She didn't open her eyes. She gave no indication to whoever was watching that anything about her state had changed. Her breathing was even, and she tried not to be relieved that the air around her was fresher than normal.

They weren't on the ship anymore.

What kind of hell planet had she landed on?

It wasn't the first. Or even the third. Back then, she'd had some sort of hope that one day she might be rescued. But she was on the wrong side of the galaxy, so far from home that no one could ever find her.

Kenzie.

Her sister's name whispered through her mind, and she shoved it away. Kenzie was back on Earth. Or maybe still working on that colony. Did she even know Carise was gone?

It didn't matter.

She could hear sleeping people, but nothing sounded like a guard, so she risked cracking her eyes open. She was on the floor with a person beside her, and her back faced open space. Carise wanted to turn over and see what was behind her, but she couldn't risk moving, not yet.

How long had she been asleep? Her last memory was a laboratory that had been all bright lights and white surfaces.

Now she seemed to be in a warehouse.

She'd gotten used to losing time, to going to sleep in one place, on one planet, and waking up somewhere completely different. The first time it had happened, she'd cried for hours. Now she just wondered how much this place was going to suck.

Her eyes adjusted to the dim light and Carise moved carefully, looking around while making it look like she was only stretching. Nothing stopped her from sitting up. There were no cries of warning, no curses or crude promises from a guard.

She counted three other people on the ground beside her, and they looked human shaped. One of them had blue skin, but the other two could have been from Earth; one was light brown like her, the other pale white and a bit blotchy. Hopefully they weren't on a desert planet—that skin looked like it would burn fast.

The three people were sleeping soundly, probably drugged. Carise's brain was fuzzy around the edges, so she'd probably been drugged as well. Whoever was keeping them must have assumed they'd sleep with no need for guards. The three on the ground slept like the dead. They wouldn't wake anytime soon.

Carise could escape.

The thought was barely a whisper at first. She'd tried to escape before. It only led to pain and blood. But this time, something felt different. No one was watching her. She could spot a door with light peeking out from under it.

The worst they could do was kill her. How bad would that be?

She had nothing to lose. That thought itself set her free before she even stood up. So what if they struck her down? She'd been in chains for years by now. At least in death they couldn't torture her anymore.

Carise had to run. This could be her last, her *only* chance.

She stopped thinking, stopped doubting. And she didn't move with caution. There were no guards that she could see, but if there was some invisible camera watching overhead, she didn't want to give her observers extra time to react.

She sprang to her feet and ran for the door, crashing into it with bone rattling force. It was locked. Of course it was, but it shuddered under her weight. Carise reared back and banged into it again, and this time something gave. Two swift kicks were enough to pry open a hole big enough for her to slip through.

She saw the sky overhead. The air around her was dusty, but she was *outside*. She darted down the street, sure that someone would send up a call to stop her, but it was silent behind her. No one looked her way as she ran.

It was daylight out, but the sun was setting. Eventually she slowed down to take in her surroundings.

This wasn't Earth, that was for certain. Even in daylight she could see this planet's fat moon hanging in the sky, too big and bright to be the moon of home. The buildings seemed to be constructed from a combination of wood, mud, and brick. They looked sturdy enough, but some were falling down in disrepair.

She could hear people talking, a cacophony of what should have been unfamiliar voices and languages. But one of her captors had fitted her with a universal translator. Now there wasn't a language in the galaxy that Carise couldn't understand. There was a hollow feeling in Carise's heart as she thought of that. She'd worked so hard to learn Spanish in school, and now it was like that work was for nothing.

Not the point.

The few people milling around on the street were taller than average humans. She'd guess between six and a half and seven and a half feet tall. At five-four, she felt like a shrimp.

No, not five-four anymore. One of those damned experiments had lengthened her legs and torso by at least three inches. She'd probably be taller than Kenzie now.

She bit back a gasp of pain at the thought of her sister. Not the time. She still wasn't safe.

If she could ever *be* safe.

Other than their height and bodybuilder-esque musculature, the aliens on the street didn't have other non-human features. Maybe they were all hiding tentacles under their clothes or they could spit venom, but she wouldn't know *that* until it was too late.

Where *was* she? Was it somehow possible that she'd been dragged forward in time to an Earth where the humans had grown huge? Or maybe she was in some other dimension?

But no, this was just a regular planet in a regular galaxy. Evolution was tricky, and a lot of aliens looked weirdly alike. She knew that.

The drugs were still making her head fuzzy.

Carise was barefoot and feared that would be an issue soon. The road beneath her feet was made of dirt, and she was sure she'd step on something sharp before long. Her luck had to run out sometime. She wore a short, gray smock that looked a bit like a hospital gown and was made of the scratchiest fabric she'd ever felt, and she had a small, dark shawl that was the closest thing she had to a blanket. But at least she was clothed. She had a feeling running down these streets naked wouldn't be a good idea.

Her stomach growled. When was the last time she'd

eaten? She had no idea. She didn't know if she'd been in stasis for the journey here or if she'd merely been drugged. If she'd just woken from stasis, she'd need food soon; she'd learned *that* the hard way the first time she'd woken up under the control of strange aliens.

She'd attempted a hunger strike and nearly died in agony.

That made her path clear. She headed towards the group she could hear talking and hoped there would be shops or restaurants, or maybe a kind family who would take pity on a starving human. Or she could dumpster dive. Whatever it took to get food in her belly.

She stepped on a sharp rock and winced. Yup. Her luck was running out.

Carise walked slowly through an alley and saw tents set up in the street beyond it. There were a lot of the tall aliens walking around between the tents and tables, chatting and smiling.

A market. Almost like home.

Did they offer free samples?

She had no idea if free samples were a universal concept across the galaxy, but she sent up a little prayer of hope that they were. She needed something to nibble on quickly. Her fingertips had gone numb, the first sign of stasis starvation. It only got worse after that.

No one paid much attention to her, and she wasn't the only woman in an ugly gray smock. She also wasn't the only human, though humans were vastly outnumbered by the tall aliens. What were the aliens called?

Food mattered more than terminology.

Something hot and salty tickled her senses as Carise turned to where she could see meat sizzling on a grill. Her mouth watered and her stomach grumbled. On the table in front of the meat were an assortment of pastries that looked just as delicious as something she'd see in a shop in Paris.

She could practically taste it.

Could she beg for food? Would the alien at that stall take pity on her?

Before she'd decided to move, her feet were walking that way. She stopped a few feet away and looked at the food, licking her lips and trying not to drool. The pastry had so many *layers*. It would be buttery and crunchy and deliciously savory. And the orange sauce next to it smelled tangy and tempting.

The alien behind the stall turned his eyes on her and glared. A younger version of Carise would have reared back in fear, but her instincts had been damaged over the last few years.

"You got coin?" he demanded, the words rough as bristles over her skin.

Words caught in Carise's throat and she tried to say something, but all that came out was a squeak.

"No coin, no food." He poked a finger down the street. "Leave."

The numbness was crawling up her forearms now. Soon she'd start shivering, her body losing its ability to regulate temperature. All she needed was a bite of food, just a few extra calories, to pause the process.

But she wasn't going to steal it. At least not from someone so clearly expecting it from her. She shuffled away and made it to the edge of the alien's table, where she saw that one of those delicious pastries had fallen off the table and lay slightly squished on the ground.

Her stomach growled.

Carise looked over her shoulder. The alien wasn't watching her. He couldn't expect to sell that pastry. He'd basically thrown it away already.

She stooped down and grabbed it and took a big bite.

"Thief!"

2

Jaek hated the market. It was loud, crowded, and full of exiles looking for a fight. He stood out, inches taller than most of the Kru'dari around him, no matter how much he hunched. But his damned generator was on the verge of breakdown, and if he didn't purchase parts, he'd be freezing come winter.

He could have paid a runner to buy the parts, but he didn't want the hassle of explaining *exactly* what he needed only for the boy to come back with the wrong material. No, in this case it was all on him.

An older woman shoved him before continuing down the street, not bothering to apologize. Jaek tapped his money purse to make sure she hadn't stolen his coin. But, no, she was no pickpocket, she was just rude.

Maybe he should have asked Mad to go in his place. His best friend had no issue walking through the markets. He didn't have memories of being hounded through the streets or scrambling for scraps.

Jaek pushed them aside. Krudare was the past. He was never going home. Pardons for any exiles were rare, and for an unknown street rat, they didn't exist. It was fine. He just had to get used to it.

A headache threatened to bloom in the back of his head. He was low on energy. Back home it flowed through everything, a necessary part of life. Legend had it that Kru'dari died without access to the Fount, the source of energy on Krudare. Being cut off from the Fount was the special torture for exiles.

There were ways to generate energy: fighting and fucking, mostly. It wasn't the same, but it helped to sate the hunger that gnawed within them all. And Jaek hadn't had a fight or a fuck in a while.

But he wasn't going to die from a few hunger pangs. Not today.

"Thief!" The cry went up and a few heads turned towards a stall at the edge of the market.

Jaek froze, the memory of a long ago day holding him in his grasp for a second before releasing him. He'd done nothing wrong. No one knew or cared about his past here. Besides, there were few *actual* laws on Guerran. People were forced to exact their own justice.

Or their exile kings did it for them. But King Jadirel was a neglectful ruler at best, and he didn't give a shit about petty thieves.

"Thief!" the man cried again.

Jaek wanted to melt back into the background and escape before anyone noticed him. But he couldn't. Situations like this had a way of turning bad fast, and he needed to see if bloodshed could be avoided.

The crowd parted before him, and when Jaek made it to the stall, everything in his body hummed as he saw *her*.

She was bedraggled, hair frizzy and unkempt. Her gray tunic was stained and wrinkled, her brown skin edging towards gray, just like her clothes, except for the dark shawl over her shoulders. She was too skinny, and shorter than any Kru'dari. And her green eyes glowed with determination. She held a crumpled pastry in her hands, and crumbs flaked on her hollow cheeks.

She was no exile, no Kru'dari.

Human.

Yes, he'd seen some of those creatures over the years. Guerran was a dumping ground for Kru'dari exiles, but it wasn't closed off to the rest of the galaxy. For some reason, some other aliens *chose* to make their home there.

Had she?

By the looks of it, she'd been on the streets for some time. Or worse.

Words threatened to clog in Jaek's throat. He hated speaking, hated confronting angry stall owners. But she looked like she was about to fall over.

He needed to help her.

He liked helping people, but this went beyond that. Something inside him insisted that he keep her close, take care of her until she'd lost that gray look and her sickly thinness. He needed to help her get strong again.

She should have been no one to him. He wouldn't last long on Guerran if he took in every stray he passed. But this woman was his to help.

The man in the stall had a nasty looking knife in his hand and pointed it at the woman. "Thief!" he scowled again.

The woman's fingers curled even tighter around the pastry. "It—it—wa... was," she stuttered, shrinking back as the man swiped the knife her way. "Ground! On the ground!"

All of this agony over a discarded piece of bread? Jaek reached into his coin purse and flashed a credit at the man. "Will this cover the cost of your loss?" he asked. It was more than double what a fresh pastry would cost, and they both knew the man had already written off what she'd taken as a loss.

"I'll take my price out of her flesh." He leaned in closer, the knife glinting wickedly in the sunlight.

A crowd had gathered around them, curious exiles ready to watch a fight. But Jaek didn't want to fight. He wanted to get this woman away from here, get her more food and clothing, and keep her safe from trouble.

What had come over him?

He didn't know and he didn't particularly care.

He set the coin down on the table. "Take the payment and let it be done." Jaek straightened to his full height. The human woman shrank back even further as she realized he was a foot and a half taller than her.

But he was taller than the stall keeper too, and he'd always been broad. In a fight, it was clear who would win. Even if the man behind the stall kept his knife.

He didn't. He set it down and snatched up the coin. "Get out of here," he spat at the woman. "You won't like it if I see you again."

She stumbled back, but not before stuffing the rest of the pastry in her mouth and chewing madly, almost daring the man to demand she give it back.

Oh, she had spirit. Whatever she'd experienced on the streets of Orion, whatever darkness she'd witnessed, it hadn't completely obliterated the fire within her.

Jaek's energy surged, a sudden wave of exhilaration that made no sense. But he didn't have time to examine it closely. He had to get this woman away from the stall before the stall keeper got ideas.

And he had to learn her name.

They hadn't spoken a word to one another, but he wanted to. And he never wanted to speak to anyone, not even his best friend, Mad. But this woman had him eager to exchange words.

He tried to reach out and usher her away from the stall and the rest of the crowd, but she flinched. Jaek held up both hands to make it clear he wouldn't touch her again.

"My name is Jaek." He hoped she could understand him. Most humans this far away from their home planets had translators embedded in their skin to make communication possible. "How can I help you?"

She was still chewing. She wiped at her mouth with the back of her hand and then swallowed. Her breaths heaved in and out of her, her whole body moving with the motion. Jaek was mesmerized. He couldn't look away from her for anything. The king could have offered him a pardon right then and he would have said no if it meant he had to look away from this woman.

But she wasn't caught in the same spell. Her eyes darted around, and those heaving breaths came faster and faster as she began to hyperventilate.

He wanted to reach out, to try and calm her, but he'd said he wouldn't touch her and he meant to keep his promise. He really did.

Until her eyes rolled back in her head and she slumped to the ground. He darted forward to catch her.

3

Carise's stomach roiled, and her mouth felt like it was full of cotton. Rancid, rotten cotton that threatened to revolt and escape. She was laying down and she didn't know why, but she didn't open her eyes and she tried to keep her body relaxed.

Where was she?

Why was she on something... soft?

She couldn't remember the last time she'd slept on a comfortable mattress, but that was exactly what the material under her felt like. If she kept her eyes closed, she could believe the last years were some horrible dream that had kept her in its grasp for far too long. If she kept her eyes closed, she was back in her room on Earth. Her dad was downstairs cursing at the TV, not caring that she was trying to sleep.

If she kept her eyes closed, all her problems would go away.

But it didn't smell like Earth. The difference was subtle, but distinct. It was dusty and a bit metallic, not the humid green smells from home. How she even remembered the smells of Earth, she wasn't sure. Maybe she was imagining it.

And thinking about home was her brain's way of trying to protect her. Wherever she was, it was bad. Nothing good ever came from waking up in a strange place. Had she been recaptured? She remembered her escape, remembered the market and the pastry.

And the man. Well, the alien.

Then she didn't remember anything.

She heard something *clink* and flinched. Damn it. A flinch like that gave her away. Was her body stupid enough to think she was safe?

She could sense a presence near her, whoever was clinking things around. The air moved with him, or her, she supposed, but she had a suspicion about who she would see if she opened her eyes.

But was she brave enough to do so? Opening her eyes made this real.

She was in a strange alien's bed on a strange alien planet. It was a different flavor of bad than she was used to, and Carise didn't want to expand her horizons of suffering.

The alien breathed in, as if he were about to speak, then she heard a heavy exhale as if he'd given up the idea.

She couldn't keep her eyes closed all day. It was

better to face the horror now than dream up what terrible things were about to happen to her.

She opened her eyes.

The first thing she saw was rock and lots of it. There was a dome of it over the bed and the walls were chiseled out of it. It wasn't tame marble slabs used as decoration; no, this place had been carved into the land itself. But the bed was soft in contrast, and there was plenty of light in the room.

Who knew that a cave could be homey?

She turned her head and there he was, the alien from the market. Her heart gave a strange lurch and awareness sizzled through her body. Carise's fingers curled in the sheets, clutching them close. She was fully clothed, or, well, as clothed as she'd been during her escape, but she wanted the sheet for further defense.

She couldn't quite identify the heat surging through her. Rather, she *could*, but it terrified her more than any torture.

Could she *want* an alien at first sight?

He was huge. Seven feet tall, at least, maybe a few inches over that. And his muscles made her think he could tear a thick piece of steel in half, or maybe a chopped up tree trunk. He had a brown beard that had gone a bit wild, making him look like some sort of mountain man, and his brown eyes were somehow both soft and serious.

And he wasn't wearing a shirt.

Holy crap, he was hot. She wasn't looking at defined

abs or anything like that. His muscles were useful, the kind that came from hauling heavy things and working hard every minute of his life. And, she supposed, he did.

What little bits of life she'd seen on this planet didn't look easy. While this was a planet that had access to space travel, she hadn't seen much other tech among the people. Not anything she hadn't seen on Earth, at least.

Was it possible this guy was human?

No. They didn't grow humans like that.

The man—the alien—picked up a small tray and placed it on the table beside the bed. It had a clay mug full of what smelled like tea and a small plate with bread, cheese, and an unfamiliar fruit.

Carise's stomach growled. She'd devoured the pastry and staved off the worst of stasis sickness, but she was still starving. And she'd learned not to reject food, no matter who was offering it to her.

She'd worry about whether or not he'd drugged it later. She was completely in his power, so it wasn't like she had another choice.

Her hand hovered over her options and she froze. She couldn't remember the last time she'd had the opportunity to actually *choose* what she ate, even if it was just a few items on a plate. Her captors favored a flavorless, horribly textured sludge that carried all the nutrients a body needed.

This was *real* food.

She looked up at the alien again. He was watching

her with those serious brown eyes, hovering at the edge of the bed.

She pulled her legs in, holding them close as if they were some sort of shield.

The alien took a step back. "It's just food." His voice was low and scratchy, as if he didn't talk much. "I didn't do anything to it."

She looked back at the plate and tried to choose. Why was it so *hard?* Had all those bastards who'd tried to own her really broken her of such a simple thing? Frustration backed up in her throat and she wanted to scream, but the idea of making such a noise terrified her.

What if she accidentally called down vicious guards?

But the tall alien was the only person there.

He took a step towards her, and Carise froze. She couldn't fight him, not even if her brain wasn't stalled in terror. Not even Kenzie could take this guy out.

What would Kenzie think of her if she saw her now?

For once, Carise was glad her sister was light years away. She didn't want Kenzie to see what she had become.

He reached out a hand slowly and picked out a slice of cheese. "It's safe," he said, and slowly ate it. "See?"

That wasn't the problem, but he didn't know that. And though it wasn't his intention, the alien's action broke Carise out of her rut and she reached for the cheese. She didn't taste the first slice, she ate it so fast. Nor the second. But she stopped to chew when she got to the third small slice, savoring the sharp bite as it practically melted on her tongue.

She finished the rest of the cheese and looked at the alien.

He grabbed a slice of the fruit and ate it. She followed right after and finished it. That left only the bread. And when he grabbed for it to take his safety bite, Carise pushed past him and snatched up the small loaf for herself.

"Mine." She bared her teeth and held the bread to her side, daring him to take it. He was *huge*, he didn't need the food. But her growling stomach still wasn't satisfied.

Strangely, that made the alien smile. And her stomach did a weird flippy thing that had nothing to do with food. What the hell was going on?

Carise pushed her concerns aside as she stuffed the bread into her face. It wasn't pretty and she probably showered the bed in crumbs, but she didn't care. She'd slept in much worse places.

When she was done with the bread, she drank the tea and was surprised at the sweetly herbal flavor. Hibiscus? Some weird space plant? She didn't care. It quenched her thirst and that was enough.

Once she finished, the alien gathered up her plates and took them away. He was only gone for a minute before he came back and pulled a stool up and sat beside the bed.

Was he her savior or her jailer? Or both?

Carise was too scared to ask. Curiosity killed the

abducted human. She'd seen it before and learned her lesson without being told. She hated how weak it made her feel to sit meekly by and try and decipher what her captors were doing by their actions, but brave women got killed.

She was still alive.

And she had no intention of dying.

"My name is Jaek," he said, and it echoed in her mind. He'd said it before, back in the market. He hunched in on himself as he leaned forward, but nothing could disguise just how big he was. "This is my home. You're safe here." He paused and looked at her expectantly.

Carise stared back. She wasn't sure if she should talk.

"Can you understand me?" he asked, speaking very slowly. "Do you have a translator?"

She answered with a nod, and then a weak "Yes," when she realized a nod might not mean the same thing on this planet.

Jaek smiled and it changed his face. He seemed to light up from the inside, his brown eyes edging toward gold and several years melting off of him until she wondered if he was possibly close to her age.

How old was she?

She didn't know how long ago she'd been taken, but it wasn't long after her twenty-second birthday. Years, probably. But how many?

If she let her mind wander down that path, she'd go crazy.

"What's your name?" Jaek asked, when she subsided back into silence.

He cared about her name? She'd clung to it fiercely in her time in captivity. Some of her captors didn't seem to mind, while others staunchly referred to her however they wanted.

And Jaek was asking. He'd fed her and asked her what her name was.

Could he possibly be safe?

She was fooling herself to believe it.

But she had to answer. She couldn't fight him if he got mad. "Carise. Carise Fletcher." She braced herself for his reaction. She couldn't stop him if he refused to call her by her name. She couldn't do anything but remain determined to remember who she was.

Jaek nodded. "Carise." There was bit of a lilt to his pronunciation, a heavy emphasis on the *i* that she'd never heard before. But he was saying her name and she liked it.

"Jaek," she said, acknowledging his. And he smiled again.

She liked his smile.

She wanted to say more, but a yawn caught her off guard and her mouth opened so wide that her jaw cracked. The covers around her were warm from her body heat and it was so comfortable she could slip back down and sleep for hours.

"Sleep," said Jaek. "We'll talk more later."

She wasn't sure she wanted to talk. And maybe she

should have wanted more answers. But her body needed sleep, and so she succumbed.

Dreams had long ago abandoned her. Or maybe she just didn't remember them. Carise was happy for that.

She'd never rest again if nightmares hounded her. But strangely, that night she wasn't afraid of nightmares. Not with a giant alien hulking beside her bed, ready to feed her and keep her safe.

How strange.

4

Carise woke up exactly where she'd gone to sleep. A strange luxury. Old habit made her keep her eyes closed as she listened for threats in her surroundings. She did hear someone moving around, but quickly realized it was Jaek.

He was safe.

At least for now.

She opened her eyes and sat up. The stool beside the bed was empty, and she had something approaching privacy for the first time in a long time. She didn't know what to do with it. She was in a strange alien's home, light years away from Earth. The only reason she might take advantage of her privacy was to cry.

And Carise had run out of tears a long time ago.

She sat up and scowled as her tunic scratched her skin. The thing was filthy and she could smell it, always a bad sign. Did Jaek have a shower she could use? Could she ask?

Would he want to join her?

She swallowed past a lump in her throat. Yes, he was hot. Yes, her body had reacted to him. But that didn't mean she wanted him to take advantage. What if he expected it for his help? It wasn't like she had anything she could use to pay him back except her body.

Her breaths came in fast and her fingers tingled. She had to get herself under control. She couldn't remember the last time she'd hyperventilated before yesterday, and now it had happened twice. She'd be killed if she didn't stop it.

It took longer than it should have and by the end, Carise's hands were shaking. But her breathing was under control and Jaek seemed to be none the wiser. He hadn't come to check on her yet.

She pushed the blankets off of herself and swung her legs over the side of the bed. The stone floor was covered in thick furs and carpets, but her feet were still chilled. Fuzzy slippers would have been welcome, but Carise put her personal discomfort out of mind. She'd suffered worse.

And her ragged shawl was sitting on the edge of the bed. It wasn't slippers, but it helped. It was a cheap piece of fabric, mass produced in the Oscavian Empire and liable to fall apart with even the gentlest use. But it had kept Carise warm during her last bout of captivity and she was happy for that.

She wrapped it around herself and went to find Jaek.

She passed by a couch with disturbed pillows and a rumpled blanket on it. So that was where Jaek had slept. The couch was big, but it couldn't have been comfortable for the giant alien.

The least Carise could do was give him his bed back. The couch would fit her just fine.

She smelled food and followed her nose to a small kitchen. Jaek stood over a burner where a pot emanated savory scents that made her stomach rumble. If she ate too much of his food, she'd be ruined for the meal paste she'd survived on for so long.

Good. Carise wasn't going back. She'd rather die than be captured again.

Jaek turned around and smiled when he saw her. "You're awake. Good. This will be ready in a moment." He set out two bowls, and once the food was finished, filled them to the brim before setting one before her with a huge spoon.

Carise wasn't sure she could fit the whole spoon in her mouth, but she'd try. It smelled so good she'd figure out a way to eat stew with her hands if she had to.

But the spoon fit. Barely. And she gobbled down the meal before Jaek had finished half of his. He glanced at her empty bowl and then silently filled it with more stew from the pot.

She ate until she was full, a strange luxury she knew she shouldn't grow used to. But Jaek seemed determined to fill her up.

She wasn't complaining.

He took her bowl once they were both done and placed them in a small sink in the corner of his tiny kitchen. For such a big cave, he hadn't given much space to cook. Maybe he didn't like it.

She wouldn't insult his home by asking, though. Not while he was feeding her.

"You can clean up in there." He pointed towards a small doorway in the back of the cave. "Hot water. Soap. I can clean your clothes."

Carise looked down at her tunic and felt her cheeks flame. "Um..." Telling him she was naked under the scratchy fabric might give him ideas she wasn't sure she wanted him to have, even if he was the most attractive man—alien—she'd ever seen.

He realized her predicament without her needing to say more. "Right. New clothes." He shot across the room and opened a small wardrobe, pulling out a plush black robe. "This will keep you warm. We can get more later."

More? Well, she wouldn't say no to something that *didn't* scratch her skin raw. And when she took the robe from him, she had to bite back a sound of pleasure from how soft it was.

She took her time in his giant shower. Everything of his was giant, but at least this time she didn't feel like a small child while she stood under the heat of the water. She felt like she was in some magical cavern, a secret princess being cared for by a recalcitrant woodsman.

She only hoped she didn't end up devoured by some

wolf. Though she might have been mixing up her fairy tales.

It took her a long time to scrub away the grime. Dirt was embedded in her skin, but that wasn't the entire problem. Once she started scrubbing, she couldn't stop. Not when she remembered every dastardly thing that had been done to her since she'd been abducted. She wanted it all washed away in the water, and she'd wash her skin until blood ran if that was what it took.

But things didn't work that way. *That* grime was embedded in her brain. A little soap couldn't fix it.

She was as clean as she could get, but she still stood under the water for a few more minutes.

Eventually she had to step out. Or become a fish. Since she was pretty sure fish didn't get to eat delicious stew, Carise turned the water off and used a towel hanging on a hook over the door to dry off.

Her hair was a mess. She'd need a comb and a lot of patience to deal with it. She was almost grateful one of her captors had shaved her nearly bald. *Almost*. Now her hair was a few inches long, tangled in knots and threatening to mat. If it had been longer, she would have had to cut it off and start again anyway. It wasn't like alien captors cared much about temperamental hair.

Once she was dry, she pulled the robe on and hugged herself in its soft embrace. Jaek wasn't getting this back. No way. It was too comfortable.

She couldn't remember the last time she'd worn something so soft.

Jaek didn't ask her any questions when she stepped out of the shower. Nor when she sat down on his rumbled couch and stared into the fire pit that had been carved into one wall. Was there a hidden chimney? Or was it some sort of alien technology that stopped the room from getting smokey?

He didn't talk at all, and Carise was grateful. She wasn't sure what she would say. She didn't want to list out all that she'd gone through. She didn't want his pity.

And she didn't want him to learn enough so he could sell her back to her previous captors.

That had happened once. Her first and only other true escape attempt. She'd thought she'd found safety with a strange purple alien who claimed he'd help her get home. Then he'd led her straight back to the slave market.

Jaek wasn't acting like that guy. But that didn't mean she could give him all her trust.

A few hours must have passed in silence before Jaek stood. "I need to go out. Will you be okay alone?"

"Yes." It was on the tip of her tongue to ask him to get her some new clothes and a comb for her hair, but she bit it back. He'd given her so much already. She couldn't make requests.

Jaek stared at her for another minute before nodding and leaving without another word.

And that left Carise alone.

Should she escape?

The question whispered through her mind. Jaek had

been nothing but kind to her, but kindness could hide the worst of intentions. She didn't know where he was going. And he could come back with people who meant her harm.

Or he could be attending to normal business. Maybe he had a job. Was he late for his shift? Did they even *have* shift work on this planet?

Carise pushed herself off the couch and paced. Every minute she dithered was a minute wasted. But the bed had been soft. The robe was a dream. And he'd fed her more than once.

She'd become a freaking cheap date.

Had he even spoken more than twenty words to her?

She wasn't going to run. She'd used up her bravery already, running from her previous captors. But she did approach the entrance and test the door. It was locked, but she was able to unlock it and swing the door open. Outside there were piles of sticks propped up against the rock and some had fallen when she opened the door.

There was no hint of the city. She saw barren rocks and sand, and, in the distance, short trees with gnarled branches.

Were they even on the same planet where she'd stolen from the market?

Did it matter?

Carise closed the door and locked it again. At least Jaek didn't seem to be holding her prisoner. She could walk away right now and make her way to...

Where?

She didn't know where she was. She had no money. And her captors might be looking for her. If she left Jaek's house she'd be in an even worse place than she was now.

But she had to talk to Jaek. She had to figure out where she was and what to do next.

Could she figure out a way to go home?

She snooped around Jaek's things but didn't find anything interesting. Eventually she curled up on his couch, pulled the blanket over herself, and fell asleep.

She woke the next morning in the big bed. Jaek lay on the couch, his body contorted trying to fit and still half-falling off. She watched him for a moment and then tore her gaze away. She wasn't about to get caught staring at Jaek.

He might want things.

So might she.

He was gorgeous. He'd rescued her. And he'd been a perfect gentleman ever since. Would it be so bad to invite him into the bed and see what he could do to her?

Yes. Yes, it would be. Whatever her body was feeling didn't matter. She wasn't about to jump into bed because she felt a bit grateful. That wasn't her. At least, it wasn't the person she'd been back on Earth.

And Carise didn't want to find that she'd changed *that* much.

Jaek blinked his eyes open while she was still looking at him, and he smiled. She really liked his smile.

"Good morning," he grunted out as he maneuvered

into a sitting position. He tried to hide a wince, but Carise saw it.

"You should sleep in your own bed." Carise made sure she was wrapped up neatly in her robe before she stood. She didn't want to flash the alien. "I can sleep on the couch. Until..."

"Sleep in the bed. You need it more." His tone was harsh and she flinched, but he didn't see it. He was already standing. "Let's get breakfast down the street. There's a good food stall."

Carise looked down at herself and then back at Jaek. "I'm not exactly wearing clothes."

He sucked in a ragged breath and froze where he stood. His chest heaved and he seemed to be moving through molasses when he turned to her, but his expression was neutral. "Your tunic is clean. Or you can wear the robe. No one will mind."

What kind of place *was* this planet?

Carise hugged the robe close, savoring its soft feel. But she decided to change into her tunic instead. She didn't want to risk anything happening to her new favorite piece of clothing.

"We'll get you more clothes later," Jaek promised.

An unwelcome weight settled over Carise's shoulders. "I can't pay you back. I don't have any money. And I've put you out of your own bed. Why—" She cut herself off, but the question had already escaped.

Jaek took two steps towards her and bent down, hunching his shoulders so he wasn't quite so tall.

Though nothing could completely get rid of the height difference. "You needed help."

Was that *it?* She'd crossed the galaxy and just happened to run into a good Samaritan? She couldn't believe it. Jaek *had* to have some kind of ulterior motive. Everyone did. And she'd have to remain on her guard, otherwise he might betray her.

With that thought in mind, she followed him out the door and watched as he rearranged the branches and leaves around the entrance until it was fully obscured. He didn't mention that it must have been obvious that she'd opened the door while he was gone the day before.

Maybe he didn't care.

Or maybe he was waiting for her to get comfortable.

The area where his cave home was located looked like the wilderness, but they'd only walked for about five minutes when they reached the edge of a settlement where a handful of shops and stalls were set up. There weren't many people around, but those that were were all as tall as Jaek. She hated feeling so short. Maybe she'd insist he buy her a pair of stilettos when he found her clothes.

She had to bite back a smile at the image that conjured up. Carise could wear heels, sure, but anything higher than three inches was liable to crack her ankles in two.

Jaek led her to a stall and ordered filled pastries from the baker. They stood at a table a few feet away and ate.

Carise's was still steaming when he handed it to her, the savory meat inside inviting her to take a giant bite.

She ate so fast she barely tasted it, but Jaek was right there, ready with another for her to eat slower this time.

It was as good as he promised.

Could he *really* be helping her just because she needed help?

The baker called him back and Jaek left her at their table. Carise took the opportunity to look around while she slowly savored the rest of her pastry. The street looked wrecked. The buildings were made of some kind of sandy stone and wood. One of the buildings was a complete ruin, collapsed in a heap with only a tarp acting as a roof. And yet, she saw people moving inside the wreckage.

The other buildings were in disrepair. Some had boarded up windows. Others had glass, but most of it was broken. Many of the windows were nothing more than empty holes in pockmarked stone.

She was glad for Jaek's cave. It was sturdier than anything she'd ever seen.

But the people on the street didn't seem worried about the disrepair of the neighborhood. They smiled and spoke to one another and went about their business like nothing was wrong.

A hush fell down one end of the street and Carise's heart sank. She knew something was wrong, knew this nice breakfast was too good to be true. At the end of the street a hulking alien who looked just a *little* bit like Jaek, huge and dark haired and wearing battle leathers, stalked down the road, carrying a strap of leather in one hand.

The strap was a leash and it led where it wrapped around a human throat. The human stumbled behind the alien, bruised and wearing torn clothes and looking miserable.

The alien looked at Carise and smiled.

Panic overtook her and Carise ran.

5

JAEK HAD ONLY SPOKEN to Endryx for a moment before the street grew quiet. It happened from time to time and it usually meant trouble.

He wasn't in the mood for trouble, not today. Carise was scared of her own shadow and he wanted to show her that not every place on Guerran was going to hurt her. Though he wasn't sure how much of that he exactly believed.

Guerran wasn't a place for the weak.

But Carise wasn't weak. She might have been frail and damaged, but she'd survived horrors he could only imagine. Or so he thought. He didn't have the story from her, but he didn't think he needed it. Her scars told it well enough.

He glanced down the street and scowled as Baryn strutted with a human on a leash. The man thought he was important ever since he'd done a favor for Jadirel, this district's exile king. Was the human a gift from Jadirel? Or was Baryn trying to show off his wealth?

Jaek wanted to stalk towards him and free the human at once. He could take Baryn out with a single punch, drink up all the energy that swirled around in him, and let the human go on his way.

But Baryn never walked without friends. His crew had to be out there somewhere.

And Jaek couldn't save everybody. Feeling sick to his stomach, he looked back to where he'd left Carise.

The table was empty.

His head whipped around, eyes darting every which way to see where she'd gone. Had one of Baryn's cronies snuck up on her and dragged her away? Had someone else?

But no. If someone had tried to take her, she would have made a sound. He was sure of it. She had to know he would do whatever it took to keep her safe.

What if she hadn't been *able* to make a sound? A hand over her throat or a quick acting sedative could keep her silent. And there were too many things the predators of Guerran could do to a helpless human.

"Hey!" Endryx called, summoning his attention.

Jaek wanted to ignore him. He needed to find Carise. Now. But Endryx had been facing her way. Maybe he'd seen something. Jaek spun around, his face a mask of anger. "Where is she? What happened?"

"She ran." Endryx shrugged as he said it, uninterested in Jaek's theatrics. Getting interested, getting involved, usually led to pain and suffering. But nothing could make Jaek back away.

"Ran where?" He bit the words out, jaw clenched and certain that every second he wasted was a second where Carise was in danger. She wasn't made for Guerran. She needed to be protected. She needed *him* to protect her.

And still she'd run.

Endryx flicked a finger down a narrow street. "That way."

Jaek didn't bother interrogating him anymore. He was losing precious time. He took off, running even though he knew it would bring attention down on him. He couldn't care right now.

He had to find Carise.

The street was more like an alley, and Jaek slammed into a wall when he didn't take a corner sharply enough. Pain radiated up his arm, but he ignored it. Hunger gnawed within him, the desperate need for energy that always existed on Guerran. It wouldn't kill him, not yet, but if he didn't replenish his resources soon, he'd be no use to Carise.

He'd have to fight.

Or fuck.

But if he thought of that now, he'd never find Carise. He couldn't think of her and fucking in the same breath. Not when she was so fragile. Not when he was responsible for protecting her.

And yet.

No.

He pushed through the thought and burned his energy like he had some to spare. Flashes of possible futures for Carise assaulted him as he imagined what could be done to her. She'd been lucky once, finding him in the market. But there weren't that many good people on this forsaken planet.

She wouldn't get lucky again.

Anything could be happening to her. She could be bleeding out already, robbed for coin she didn't have, or assaulted for something worse.

Jaek turned another corner and skidded to a halt.

Carise was there. And she was fine.

She knelt in front of a large dog, a smile bright on her face as she scratched behind its ears. The dog was putty in her hands, quite the feat for a Kru'dari Hunting Beast. They were renowned for their training and ability to take down a Kru'dari in a single bound.

And Carise had tamed it with a touch.

Jaek could sympathize.

She turned, a smile painted across her face. It dropped when she saw him. She didn't stand. But her fingers stopped petting the dog and the dog whined. "I found a puppy," she said.

Jaek eyed the dog. It was at least a hundred and fifty pounds, maybe more, with a surprisingly shiny black coat under the dust of the road, pointed ears, and a stocky body made completely of muscle. "If that *puppy* stands up on his back legs, he'll be as tall as you." And if it felt threatened... There were more dangers on Guerran than he'd thought about.

Carise gave the dog a final pat and stood.

Down the street they heard a whistle, and the dog stood at attention. He gave Carise a quick look before trotting towards the whistle and leaving them behind.

The interlude with the dog had drained some of the pounding emotion in Jaek's veins. He hated to think what he would have done without the animal. Would Carise have run from him again if he'd yelled at her?

Yes.

Definitely.

And there would be no bringing her back.

He had to keep his calm. He couldn't let Carise go. But he didn't own her. He just wanted to keep her safe.

"You ran." Tension lay heavy in his voice, and she heard it. She practically vibrated with it. But she stayed where she was.

They were both trying.

"There was a man. With another man on a leash." She glanced over her shoulder, perhaps looking for the dog. Did that kind of creature give her comfort?

Jaek could find her an animal. Or he could be an animal to protect her. "His name is Baryn. He's a detestable creature who's favored by the local exile king. And as for that... display," Jaek spat. "I wish I could do more to stop it, but every tiny section of this miserable planet is ruled by a different king. And if they say it is permissible..."

"So you'd let some despot put a leash on me." She backed up half a step, eyes darting around, looking for an escape.

"*No*," he said roughly. More wanted to come out, but Jaek feared the vehemence would scare her. He had to pull it back. "I won't let that happen."

"Why? It's not like you know me." She was defiant, and still backing away.

"Is it not enough that it's wrong?" Seeing people in chains disgusted him. He'd done as much as he could to free who he could, but there were always more people shipped in. Guerran was a convenient depot for that kind of monstrosity. The Kru'dari king didn't care, the few guards back in the Green Zone were paid to look the other way, and the exile kings were often paid in bodies.

And it was everyone else who suffered.

Apparently his reason wasn't enough. "I haven't given you anything in return," she said. "I can't pay you. You've given me *your bed* and food and shelter. People don't do that." She'd stopped backing away, probably because if she moved another foot, she'd be in the muddy street.

"I saw you and I had to help. I wish I could give you a better answer. I don't want your money, I don't care that you're in my bed." *Liar.* "I'll keep you safe for as long as you need it. If you'll allow it." He needed her to allow it. He needed her back in his home, in his life. He didn't know what instinct was driving it. *Liar.* But he just needed *her*.

There was one instinct. One want.

But that wasn't something he could even begin to imagine. Not when Carise still trembled in fear. He couldn't make demands of her. He couldn't even make requests.

"Let's head home," he offered, holding out his hand. He'd had bigger plans for today, wanting to find new clothes for her and a pair of shoes. But this outing had been exciting enough. Clothes could wait.

She eyed his hand warily for a moment, but eventually reached out and put her fingers in his. Her skin was softer than he imagined and a bit cool. He wanted to pull her close and warm her up, but he was satisfied with only her hand.

For now.

Energy danced on his fingertips. Humans were full of it. That was a reason the exile kings and their favored minions kept them around. A Kru'dari could suck a human dry over the course of months and feel almost as full as the Fount back home made them. Others were more patient and let humans recover their energy between feedings so the humans didn't turn into empty husks.

Jaek would not take from Carise.

But, strangely, he didn't have to try. A whisper of her energy snaked up his arm without him doing a thing to summon it. He tried to block it off. It was her energy, not his. Nothing he could think of stopped it. She didn't seem to notice, and she didn't pull her hand away.

If he dropped the contact, he guessed the pull would stop. But he didn't want to let go of her hand. He soaked up her touch as he slowly led her back down the winding streets to the edge of this section of the city and towards the out lands of his home.

There was no sign of Baryn and no other obviously enslaved humans. It was only an illusion of freedom, but for now it was enough.

At the entrance to his house, Jaek knew something was wrong. The branches had been disturbed and one of his security sensors was lit, warning him.

He dropped Carise's hand. "Back up behind those rocks over there," he said, pointing. "There's a tarp you can pull over you for cover. If I'm not back in a half hour..." Should she run? Should he tell her to go to one of his few friends? Who could he even trust?

"What's wrong?" Carise asked, a tremble in her voice.

"Someone's been in my house."

6

It turned out Carise didn't have to hide for long. She hadn't even pulled the tarp over herself when Jaek stalked over to her, his face a wash of restrained anger. He said nothing to her, but she still wanted to flinch.

Was this leftover wrath from her run? She wouldn't apologize for trying to survive. Her instincts had kept her alive this long, and those instincts demanded she flee when she saw a person being dragged on a leash.

She refused to have a leash put on her own neck.

She wished she had the dog back with her. At one time she might have been scared of such a fierce creature, but it could protect her from many of the horrors of this terrible planet.

And so could Jaek.

Despite his clear anger, she followed him back to his cave. He plucked a note from a table and crumpled it in his fist before throwing it across the room.

A question lodged in her throat, but she was afraid to bring attention to herself. Jaek had been nothing but kind to her so far. He'd saved her in the market. He'd shepherded her home when she was scared. He'd given her food and a place to sleep.

But people's moods shifted on a dime. Would his?

She found her voice after a moment. "Is something wrong? Do you know who was here?" She wasn't sure she had any right to ask, but she wanted to know. She *wanted* to have that right. Jaek was letting her stay, which meant she should at least know if his cave was still safe.

He paced the room and stooped to pick up the note he'd thrown before placing it in the trash. "Our visitor was my friend, Mad."

Carise stayed on the other side of the room. Anger thrummed in Jaek, and she didn't want to be its outlet. She was close to the door. She supposed she could run. But she'd already run once today and she didn't want to be that person. Her instincts had kept her alive, but she couldn't keep living like this. Not forever. She had to face fears when she could.

She could face Jaek.

From a distance.

"Who is Mad? Why are *you* mad?" Surely a visit from a friend was welcome. And then something occurred to her. "It's not me, is it? You're not... hiding me?" She didn't want her captors to know where she was, but she didn't think there was likely to be any kind of search party.

As Jaek had said, human life came cheap on Guerran.

Jaek stopped pacing, but his jaw twitched and he was still scowling. "Mad is my best friend."

Carise bit back a quip and was surprised she had to do so. But she wouldn't want *her* best friend to talk about her in that tone.

Of course, she'd never see her best friend Janelle again.

"You remember what I said about exile kings?" Jaek asked, and he sounded pained.

She wasn't going to like this. Carise nodded.

He braced himself as if *she* could hurt him. "I work for one. That's how it goes on Guerran. Whatever territory you're in, you do what your exile king says. Usually that means Jadirel sends me on errands or to scare someone who isn't cooperating. He doesn't tug too tightly on my leash—fuck," he said, spinning towards her, anger and regret written across his features. "I'm sorry. That was a stupid thing to say."

Any other man and Carise would have been afraid. No question. Jaek was huge and could be loud, and he had a look that meant business. And yet she had a fundamental certainty that he wouldn't hurt *her*.

Space really had screwed up her brain.

"It's okay," she said. She tried to put the image of that man on the leash out of her mind, even though she knew it would be dancing in her nightmares for, well, ever. "And your friend works for this guy too?"

Jaek gave a tight nod. "He runs interference. He

thinks I don't know, but I'm not stupid. But I'll have to go into the city soon enough and pay my respects, otherwise Jadirel might make things unpleasant."

"And is that the same man who," she swallowed hard past a lump in her throat, "*awarded* the alien we saw today?"

"Yes."

Now Jaek wasn't looking at her and Carise knew why. He'd been treating her like she was fragile ever since he'd brought her here. He probably expected her to run again. And this time he'd let her go. Because he didn't think she would want to be near him anymore.

Carise wasn't exactly sure what her feelings were. The thought of Jaek working for such a hateful man made her stomach roil. But she'd seen and heard enough about this little planet that she understood there wasn't much choice.

Jaek could have put a leash on her. She had no way to stop him. Instead he'd fed her and kept her safe. He'd chased after her when he thought she was in danger.

And he set her body alight.

For days it had been blossoming within her, the need for him. Sleeping in his bed, even as she did it alone, didn't help. She could imagine he was right there beside her, especially when she slept in the indent left from his body. She imagined his lips and his hands on her, bringing her to the heights of pleasure with a care belied by his size.

And the size *was* intimidating. Would he even fit?

But she wanted to see. Wanted to try.

And that scared the shit out of her.

Here Jaek was, telling her an uncomfortable truth, something that should have sent her running. He worked for a man who awarded his faithful employees with *people*. No matter what else Jaek did, she shouldn't ignore that. But it was also clear that Jaek hated the man.

She knew what it was to be stuck.

She crossed the room so she stood in his shadow, but somehow he didn't make her feel small, despite the height difference. No, when she was beside him, she felt protected.

Of course, she'd need a stool if she wanted to feel anything else.

"What would you do if you could get rid of him?" She grabbed Jaek's hand and traced her fingers over the small scars and callouses on his palm. Jaek's fingers curled around hers, pulling her closer.

He didn't have to think for long. "I don't want to rule. But if I had to, I'd want to make this territory a safe haven. No one starving. No one living in vermin infested hovels. Just... safe."

It was so simple. And so impossible. On a lawless place like Guerran, he'd have to fight for every inch of peace. And what kind of peace could last under those circumstances?

She lifted his hand and brushed her lips against it.

"Cari..." Jaek's eyes went dark and he sucked in a ragged breath.

She didn't normally like nicknames, not when she'd tried so hard to hold onto her own identity over the years. But when Jaek said her name like that, it made her shiver. "I want to kiss you," she told him, summoning all her bravery. With another man she might have just gone on her tiptoes and done it.

With Jaek's height, no kissing could be done without a bit of teamwork.

And she wanted to be part of his team.

He groaned out some kind of surrender and cupped her cheek with his free hand, bending down and capturing his lips with her own. Carise gasped into it and his tongue slid in.

This was no hesitant kiss. Jaek knew what he was doing, knew what he wanted, and Carise let herself be swept away.

She clutched his arm, her fingers digging into muscle, but it didn't seem to bother him. He tasted warm and masculine, with a hint of spice from their breakfast. She could almost forget that he wasn't human. She could pretend he was just some giant fed on corn and sunshine.

She didn't want to pretend. Jaek was the one damned good thing that had come her way since she'd been taken from Earth. She didn't need to fool herself into thinking he was someone, *something*, else.

She moaned against him and shivered as he pulled her close; he had to pick her up to do it, and now she did feel small. And cherished. No boyfriend had ever had to pick her up before for a simple kiss.

Jaek did it like she was as light as a feather.

She wrapped her legs around his waist and could feel the growing evidence of his cock. Yeah. Definitely big. But she was ready for a challenge.

Was she ready right now?

Her heart stuttered, but she didn't stop kissing him. She wasn't sure what she'd do if he backed her up to his bed and tried to hitch up her scratchy tunic and have his way with her. A large part of her wanted it.

A small part of her was still scared. Not of Jaek.

Just of everything else.

Something must have tipped him off. Jaek set her down on his bed, but he didn't loom over her, didn't try and hike her clothes up.

He kissed her one last time and backed up, eyes dark and needy.

She could lean in and beg for more, push past her fears and take the pleasure she knew he would offer.

But she felt too much relief to do that. She raised her fingers up and traced her lips, wet and a bit swollen from Jaek's kiss. She wanted more. So why was she happy he'd stopped?

Jaek breathed out a harsh breath and spun away. He backed up several steps and grunted out something before rushing out the door.

Another day and Carise might have felt rejection. But

she'd seen the desire in that man's eyes. He was running away. But only to keep from taking things too far.

It shouldn't have made her smile. And yet, she fell back up onto the bed, curled into the sheets, and her face nearly split in a grin.

7

Jaek was going to go mad with lust. The kiss had opened the floodgates and now his every thought was consumed with Carise. He wanted to taste her again. Wanted to take her to bed and see if her body was as delectable as he imagined.

He wanted her to pledge herself to him and promise to stay with him no matter what.

He wanted a mate.

It was an impossible desire. A fated mate was something so rare that he didn't dare dream of one. And how could she be his fate if she'd been born on the other side of the galaxy? Surely fate wasn't so cruel.

Though they'd both ended up on Guerran.

Claiming her as his mate without the hand of fate was something Jaek couldn't inflict on her. It was a desperate bond that allowed the share of energy. But often it devolved into something despondent and dirty.

He wouldn't do that to his Carise.

She hadn't spoken to him about the kiss, though he'd caught her staring at his lips more than once. And twice now he'd had to duck into the bathroom and frantically take care of himself before she saw his problem.

She may have liked kissing him, but he'd felt the way she'd tensed against him when she felt his thickening cock. That hadn't been lust. It had been fear. And he'd cut off his own arm before he caused her another moment of it.

That meant no more kissing. Not until she was ready for it. If he kissed her again, he wasn't sure he could control himself. Not without taking drastic measures.

She'd been with him a week or so now, and he could feel his life turning around her orbit. They hadn't tried another outing into Orion. But every day, Carise seemed more and more confident. She'd wandered around the out lands around his home, exploring within sight of the door, but venturing further every day.

And still she wore that ratty tunic.

That was something he could fix.

"It's market day," he said once they'd finished their breakfast.

Carise knocked him out of the way and took the plates before he could clean them. "At least let me do the dishes," she muttered.

Jaek grinned. He'd never done anything so hopelessly domestic as this before. Perhaps he'd show Carise how to use his cooking implements. Maybe she'd like to prepare a meal or two. But not yet.

"I can go and get you better clothes. Something more comfortable." He hated the market, but he didn't tell her that. When he needed things, he hired one of the errand boys who seemed to zip through the city at all hours. But he wouldn't entrust this to someone else.

Carise fingered the edge of the robe he'd given her and Jaek felt satisfaction sink into him. He liked seeing her wearing something of his, liked providing for her. But no matter the barbaric instinct, she needed more to wear. Something colorful.

And shoes.

He'd given her lotion to help deal with the cracks in her feet that came from walking with no shoes, but he hated to see her wince as she stumbled over twigs and small rocks on her adventures in nature. There had to be *something* he could find her.

"I'm really fine," Carise insisted. "You don't need to do anything special."

He grunted. He'd build her a palace if she asked. Why couldn't he get her clothes? "Market day is the best time," he insisted. "Most options."

She looked away from him, gaze down and dejected. "I'm afraid." She was so quiet he barely heard the confession. "What if the people who took me are at the market?"

Jaek hadn't considered that. He'd spent a good deal

of time imagining what he could do to the people who'd harmed Carise, but he hadn't spent *any* time trying to hunt them down. Maybe he should fix that.

But not today.

"Stay here," he said. "I'll find something and be back soon."

"You've already done so much for me." She sounded miserable.

Jaek reached out and grabbed her hand, holding her firmly and savoring the feel of her skin next to his. "I want to. Let me."

Carise gave a tight nod, but Jaek didn't immediately let go of her hand. He wanted to pull her close and kiss her before he left.

Instead he forced himself to step back. "I'll be back soon."

He made a strategic retreat from his lodgings and walked quickly to the market. He didn't like the thought of leaving Carise alone, even though he'd done it several times before already. She was an adult. She could stand to be alone for a bit.

Nevertheless.

Market day was as crowded as usual. Jaek already felt his skin crawl even as he prowled the outer stalls, looking at vendors' wares and hoping to find something that would work for Carise.

He paused in front of a stall piled with books, scrolls, and holograms. Stories.

"Like what you see?" the vendor asked, stepping forward when Jaek didn't quickly move on. "I've stories from all across the galaxy. Standard translators mean language isn't a barrier. What do you want? Oscavian? Tol? Consortium? Earth?"

"Earth?" Jaek would have ignored the man, except Carise was from Earth. "Human stories?"

The vendor grinned, knowing Jaek was hooked. He picked up a slim volume with a dancing human figure on the front cover and curling letters that swam in Jaek's eyes. Translators took a minute to catch up with written text and they tended to give Jaek a headache. "Sixteen credits."

Jaek scoffed. "Ten."

"I'm not here to bargain," the vendor insisted, though he was still smiling.

And lying. Everything was a bargain on market day.

Jaek pulled out a ten credit note and laid it on the table. "Take it or I walk."

The vendor's eyes flicked down and then back up to Jaek. After a moment he palmed the money and handed the volume over. Jaek slid it into his satchel and moved on. He hoped Carise would like the story.

He made it, *finally*, to a vendor selling colorful dresses and tunics when a human woman bumped into him. He mumbled an apology and had to give her a second look.

Carise?

But, no. Carise was safe back home.

He hadn't gotten a good look, just seen dark hair and light brown skin. Plenty of humans looked like that. Probably. But Jaek only cared for one.

"Jaek! Hey!" Madn Damari's voice cut across the market and a few heads turned his way. Jaek wasn't a fighter, but the few times he'd gone into the pit had been bloody spectacles and few people wanted to mess with him.

Jaek wasn't in a talking mood, not even for his best friend. And he hoped if he didn't answer, Mad might go away. Perhaps it wasn't kind, but Jaek was spending more energy than he had to lose on venturing to the market. He didn't want to be here a second longer than he had to be.

But Mad was dogged. "Jaek!"

Jaek turned around and grunted a greeting. Mad just smiled at him. He'd grown used to Jaek's sometimes taciturn nature over the years. Thankfully. It was why they could be friends.

"Did you get my message?" Mad asked, eyes bright. There was a speck of something that looked like blood on his throat and he seemed brimming with energy. Had he fought? Fucked? Jaek didn't ask. He couldn't care. "Jadirel's looking for you. Did you make him angry?"

Jaek glared at the thought of Jadirel. And why did Mad assume that *Jaek* was to blame? He wanted to go home to Carise. Wanted to give her the book and a dress and see her smile. He wanted to kiss her again.

"Is everything alright?" Mad looked worried.

Jaek spent a second looking at a table full of figurines. Would Carise like these? "Need to go home." He almost picked up a figurine of a large dog but pulled his hand away. Why would she want a figurine when she could have a real dog? "Prom—" Something stopped him from mentioning Carise, though he couldn't say what. Mad was trustworthy.

But Carise was his to protect.

"Did you need to get something from the market? I could deliver it for you." Mad's voice was too gentle for Guerran, as if Jaek needed special handling.

He didn't like crowds, that didn't make him *weak*.

"It's fine," Jaek mumbled; he didn't want to waste time talking. And Mad was a good enough friend to let him get away with it. "See you later." Jaek melted into the crowd, leaving Mad standing alone.

A few minutes later he heard some kind of commotion, and it pulled several of the market goers away from usually crowded stalls. Jaek took the opportunity to purchase a bundle of clothes and call it done.

He was anxious to get home. Anxiety pounded in him, insisting that something was wrong and Carise needed him. But by the time he was back to the cave and through the door, he found Carise sitting on his couch and sketching something on a piece of paper she must have scavenged from somewhere.

She startled a bit when he closed the door, but smiled

when she saw him. He held out the bundle of clothes. "For you," he said simply.

She put her sketch aside and got up to take the clothes from him. "Thank you." There were three dresses and a pair of sandals and a bundle of underthings Jaek hadn't looked at too closely. He couldn't let himself imagine Carise wearing them. She flicked through her new clothes with a small smile on her face, pausing to pet some of the fabrics.

Jaek wanted her in colors, but he knew comfort was more important. He'd found the softest material he could, but he'd tried to make sure it would be sturdy enough to last. Of course, he could always buy her more later.

Then he remembered. "Wait," he said, even though she didn't seem like she was about to turn away.

"What?" She hugged her clothing tight to her.

Jaek reached into his bag and pulled out the book. "The vendor said it was from Earth. Thought you'd like to read." He handed the slim tome over.

She set her new clothes aside and grabbed for the book, studying the cover with a broad grin. "It's *Cinderella*."

"Have you read it?" Jaek read as many books as he could get his hands on, before bartering them in the market for more stories. But he didn't know that one.

She traced her finger over the dancing woman on the cover. "My mom used to read it to Kenzie and me before she died. When we were little. I can't believe you found this. Thank you." She stepped close, got on her tiptoes, and tilted her head up for a kiss.

Jaek couldn't resist. He leaned in and kissed her with all his heart.

If this was the greeting he got, maybe going to the market in the future wouldn't be so bad.

8

Carise had new clothes and a book. Life was looking up. For the past two days, all had been well. Jaek asked her to read to him and they'd spent half the night curled beside each other on the couch, her softly reading the story in front of her. The illustrations were different than she'd ever seen, but she liked it. A new version of something old and comfortable.

And the kisses. She liked those a lot. They just seemed to happen. They'd brush by one another. They'd stop in the middle of the story. They'd sit quietly beside one another. And whenever the urge struck, they'd kiss.

It felt new and clean and *perfect*.

But, if Carise was being completely honest, she was beginning to feel a bit cooped up. The cave was kind of small, maybe the size of a one-bedroom apartment back home. And it got daylight from somewhere, but it was still a cave. It smelled like rocks and a bit of damp.

But the thought of going outside alone made her shake. As far as she knew, there hadn't been any sign of the people who'd brought her to Guerran, the people she'd escaped from. She'd told the tale to Jaek once she could get through the story without stuttering and crying. And he'd understood. Apparently there was a level of *acceptable loss* among the slavers and one or two runaways weren't worth chasing after.

If they saw her, though, they might try to take her. And no one would stop them. No one but Jaek.

She hated to rely on him like some kind of crutch. Eventually she was going to need to figure out what to do. She couldn't just live in Jaek's cave for the rest of her life stealing kisses and remembering home.

Did she want to try and go home?

She'd stopped dreaming about Earth a long time ago. Remembering it, dreaming of it, thinking of it hurt too much when she knew she'd never go back. She'd cried her eyes out so many times in those early days that she was always shocked that she still had the ability to produce tears.

But she was free now. And a space flight back to Earth couldn't be cheap. But it *was* possible.

She didn't want to leave Jaek.

That was freaking crazy.

Her first thought should be climbing on a spaceship and going back to Earth. Kenzie had to be sick with worry. Her big sister would blame herself for Carise's disappearance. Of course, it wasn't her fault, but that rarely mattered.

Carise's dad wouldn't care. Did he even know she was gone?

She had friends back on Earth. Or at least she'd *had* friends back before she was taken. She still didn't know how long it had been. She could find out, but she was afraid. What if she found out she'd been in cryostasis for decades and everyone she knew back home was dead?

If she kept thinking about this, she'd go crazy.

She was curled up on Jaek's bed, clutching the small sketch book he'd found for her, but she hadn't been able to draw anything today. She didn't have much talent for it, but it was something to do. Jaek admired her childish chicken-scratch drawings like they belonged in the Louvre.

The guy was going to give her a big head.

But it was nice to be appreciated.

As if summoned by her thoughts, Jaek stepped into view. He was dressed in simple clothes and his shoes were on. He had a canvas bag slung over one shoulder. If she could do him justice, she'd draw him every day.

"Heading out?" she asked. He left sometimes to run errands, or maybe do his job. They hadn't spoken much about what he did for his exile king. Honestly, Carise didn't want to know. Jaek was her protector. She didn't want to find out that she needed protection *from* him.

"I want to show you something," Jaek said. "Get ready. It's a bit of a walk."

Carise put her sketch book aside and shimmied out of the bed. She still wore the robe Jaek had given her. It was more comfortable than anything else she had and there was something about the fact that it had once been Jaek's that gave her comfort. Not that she was going to admit that to him.

Maybe she was too comfortable with him. Maybe she should be more wary. But she couldn't force it. She trusted Jaek. She liked him. And she wanted to follow where he led.

For now, at least.

She selected one of her dresses, this one covered in dainty little green and blue flowers. It fell to mid-calf, and would have probably been a mini-dress on a Kru'dari woman. The sandals were a better fit, the material somehow hugging her feet like they'd been designed for her.

She did what she could for her hair, but it was still a bit of a mess. She'd forgotten to ask Jaek for a comb. She took an extra bit of fabric he had laying around and wrapped it around her head as a makeshift scarf.

There. As good as it got.

Jaek was waiting for her when she came out of the bathroom and his eyes flicked up and down, taking in the dress. It wasn't flattering. She looked a bit like she belonged on an old-timey prairie. But he seemed to like what he saw.

He held out his hand and she took it.

It was a beautiful day outside, sunny and not too hot.

Not a rain cloud in sight. Though, now that she thought of it, it hadn't rained at all since she'd arrived. "Does it rain here?" she asked as they walked down a dusty path to a copse of trees about five minutes away from the cave.

"Of course. We can get terrible flooding during the rainy season. But that's not for a couple more months." They made it to the trees and instead of staying on a path that looked like it was well traveled by people and carts, he pointed her to what looked like a dense wall of branches. But once they'd taken a few steps, she saw the narrow passage.

"Where are we going?" She wasn't worried, but she didn't want to get lost in the woods, either.

"It's a surprise," Jaek insisted.

She heard twigs snap somewhere behind them and jerked her head back, but she didn't see anything. It was probably an animal. Nothing to be worried about. Jaek certainly didn't seem to be paying any attention. Carise was too wired by what had been done to her. She didn't need to jump at every sound. But it would take time to unlearn that instinct.

She smelled water in the air a few seconds before the path widened, and they ended up at a verdant spring with a small waterfall in the distance. It was like something out of a dream. Butterflies—or whatever the Kru'dari called them, but they looked like butterflies to her—fluttered along one edge of the spring, hovering over bright pink flowers.

The water was sparkling and clear, the bottom of the spring some sort of flat rock. And the mist coming off the waterfall hit her in the face and she sighed in pleasure. It was cool, but pleasantly so.

"This is beautiful," she breathed out, the muscles in her back relaxing as she took it all in. "Wow."

Jaek set his pack down and pulled her close. "Do you like it?"

She wrapped her arms around his waist and looked up at him. "I didn't know there was anything like this on Guerran."

"It has its secret treasures." They stayed in an embrace for several moments. But eventually Jaek pulled away and knelt beside his pack, pulling out a cleverly folded blanket and carefully wrapped food and two empty cups. "We can drink from the spring," he said. "Best water on the planet."

Well, Carise had drunk worse. Though she wasn't sure she would have been willing to drink from any sort of wild spring back on Earth. But she trusted Jaek. If he said it was safe, it was.

He filled their cups and she sat down on the blanket. He sat beside her once the drinks were ready. Their legs brushed together as they picked at the bread, cheese, and fruit that made up the bulk of their meal.

"Where does the fruit come from?" she asked. "I don't think I've seen many trees, other than those we walked past in the out lands." Farmland back home stretched for miles and miles, but she hadn't been outside the city here to know anything about the rest of the planet.

"Farms outside of Orion, mostly." Orion was the city within walking distance of Jaek's cave. "And there's Aera, it's the other big city on Guerran, but they don't let many people in their dome. They do a lot of farming there and ship to Orion. The exile kings have a council that deals with food imports."

"So no one territory controls the food, right? Because that person would have too much power." She didn't need to have a political science degree to understand that.

"Exactly."

They lapsed into silence again, eating their food. And Jaek was right, the spring water tasted better than anything she'd drunk on Guerran. And possibly Earth.

"Does anyone else know about this place?" It felt like a secret, like they were the only two people on the planet. And a jealous part of her wanted to keep it that way. But what right did she have to hide this beautiful spot from anyone?

"It's not a secret," Jaek said, "but it's a hike from the city and there are other, easier spots to go to. Almost no one comes here."

"That's why you like it." Of course it was. Her Jaek liked time alone. Though he'd never begrudged a moment with her.

Was he *blushing*?

Carise tipped back her head and laughed as joy

bubbled through her. She wanted to take this moment and bundle it up so she could remember it forever. Nothing could make it better.

Or so she thought. Then Jaek pulled her close and covered her lips with his and it *truly* became perfect.

They fell backward onto the ground, Jaek looming above her, holding his body tight so he didn't squish her. She let her hands roam over him, loving the feel of his muscles under her fingers.

A few days ago, she wouldn't have been able to stand this, she knew. She'd frozen in that first kiss. But there wouldn't be any freezing anymore, not with Jaek. Not now that her heart trusted him with everything she was.

And she wanted everything he had.

His tongue swept into her mouth and she didn't try to stop the way she moaned against him. He gave everything with his kiss. The man didn't know how to hold himself back. He wasn't someone who understood the meaning of the word casual, and it was just what Carise needed.

If she was going to give her heart to anyone, he needed to want it all. And he needed to give her his heart in return. As terrifying as it was, she was almost certain Jaek would tear the organ out of his chest and present it to her if she asked.

Instead she just wanted more kisses.

Her dress hiked up and she might have felt naked, but not with Jaek. If anything, she wished he'd tear the damned thing off. He placed his knee between her legs and she grinded down on him, her body heating up with promise.

Jaek pulled back a bit and Carise tried to hold him close, but he was too strong. "Yes?" he asked.

"Yes," she said, and it came out breathy and desperate. And when Jaek leaned back down, she could feel his stiffening cock against her belly.

Yes.

She was desperate with want, growing wet and heated. And if Jaek wanted to take her right there, she'd gladly be taken. But the infuriating man didn't pull off his clothes or trail his fingers along her pussy.

He kept kissing her. Driving her mad.

And still she wanted more.

She was ready to beg before he pulled away again, but this time it wasn't to check if she was still with him. It had to be clear she was with him all the way. No, this time he slid down her body and pushed her dress the rest of the way up, baring her from the waist down to his gaze.

He stared at her spread legs for a long moment and she could feel the heat of the look. It was a bit disconcerting, being on display like that. Or it might have been if it was anyone but Jaek.

It had been a long time since she'd done this, since she was back on Earth with her last fumbling boyfriend who'd thought he was God's gift to women.

But he had nothing on Jaek, and she couldn't even

remember the last guy's name when Jaek was looking at her like she was some offering laid out on an altar.

He kissed his way over her stomach and down to her sex, making her gasp as his tongue touched her for the first time. It made her writhe, her fingers tangling in the blanket beneath her as Jaek took their feast to another level.

When they'd left for their walk, she'd never imagined that *she* would be his meal. Nor that she'd be so eager to be devoured.

Carise had been dreaming of this for days now. It was hard to do anything but when she spent her nights tangled up in his sheets, living in his house like his lover. And now that she had a taste of it, she wanted more.

His tongue swirled around her, his fingers dove into her, and her body wanted the promises his body was making to her.

The day had been nice and cool, but now she was heated inside from what felt like a sun. Her heart beat so fast she feared it would explode, and her whole body tingled. It had never felt like this before. She didn't know it was possible.

It was almost too much. Almost. The tingling grew even stronger, just until the point of pain. She didn't quite understand it, but she didn't care, not as long as Jaek stayed between her legs and showed her that he knew exactly what he was doing.

She reached her hand down and rested it on his head.

And then the strangest thing happened.

All those tingles that were making her shiver *rushed* down her arm and seemed to empty into Jaek.

What?

There was still a trickle of it, just enough to make her feel like she was fizzing with static electricity. She probably should have followed the thought. Instead, her pleasure mounted and mounted, Jaek's tongue and fingers becoming frantic as her hips pumped and she made desperate pleas for more.

Pleasure crested, her body rippling around him as she came. She cried out his name as the orgasm ripped through her. Her chest heaved and she breathed deep, trying to gain control of a body that wanted the moment to go on and on and on.

Carise surrendered to it and to Jaek. She knew he'd keep her safe. There was nothing to worry about as long as he was around.

It was a hell of a time to fall in love.

Her breathing started to even out and languor washed over her. She was already drifting off to sleep.

The last thing she heard was Jaek, but she must have been mistaken. Because she was almost sure he said, "Impossible."

9

CARISE DIDN'T KNOW how long she'd slept. It was still sunny when she blinked her eyes open, and for a second, she was worried she'd slept through an entire day. But it was probably less than an hour.

She turned over to ask Jaek, and was surprised to see he was gone.

Weird.

He'd cleaned up their picnic, wrapping up the extra food and putting it back in his bag, along with the cups. The only thing left out was the blanket.

But where was he?

She wasn't worried. Not yet. Jaek would never leave her somewhere dangerous. This was his special place and he must have thought it safe enough to leave her sleeping. He probably had snuck off somewhere to pee.

No need to worry.

But some of the wonderful relaxation she felt from

the location *and* the activities before her nap started to wear off, replaced by wariness. She felt like she was being watched and she didn't like it.

She wasn't. She couldn't be.

Or if she was, it was because Jaek was somewhere nearby.

Another few minutes went by and Carise started to actually worry. "Jaek," she called out, not quite yelling. If he was close by, he'd hear, but she didn't want anyone else to hear and think she was in distress. Distressed women didn't do well on Guerran.

No Jaek.

Okay. This was fine. Really. He was probably stretching his legs. Worst case scenario, he'd gone back to the cave for some reason and would be back shortly. It was less than a fifteen minute walk away.

Needing to do something, Carise got up and folded the blanket as best she could. There must have been some trick to it. No matter what she did, she couldn't fold it small enough so that it would fit in the bag.

Oh well. Jaek would be back soon to help her.

Her skin still prickled with the thought of being watched.

She sat at the edge of the spring and dangled her feet in the water. She spotted a couple of fish and wondered if a river or creek fed into the water. Were there oceans on Guerran? There had to be. But where?

Maybe Jaek could show her a map sometime. She wanted to know the geography of her new home.

The thought brought her up short.

Was she really thinking about staying in this lawless, desperate place?

Jaek was good, but he couldn't be that good. Right?

Well, the satisfaction in her body begged to differ.

And Guerran had its charms. Mostly in the form of her seven-foot-tall Kru'dari lover and the secret places he could show her. But it wasn't like Earth was perfect. She could make a real life here.

If she was willing to give up all hope of ever seeing her sister again.

There was a lump in Carise's throat at the thought. If there was some chance of seeing Kenzie again, or of at least letting her know that she was okay, Carise had to try. Kenzie had spent her entire life protecting Carise, and Carise couldn't let her think she'd failed.

Maybe she could get a message to Earth. That was certainly cheaper than a ride on a spaceship.

And it would give her more time to think.

Would Jaek leave Guerran if she asked him? She couldn't imagine it. This was his home. He didn't seem to have much and it was a place full of terrible people, but she couldn't just ask him to leave.

What if he said no?

What if he said *yes?*

None of it mattered if he had disappeared. She was making up fantasies. They'd all go away in a puff of smoke as soon as reality intruded. And though the spring was beautiful, Carise was finding it a bit disconcerting now that she was alone.

Were there any dangerous wild animals on Guerran? Anything more dangerous than the people? She really didn't want to get attacked by some kind of alien bear.

She whipped her head around when she heard a rustle of leaves, but there was nothing there: no Jaek, no other people, no bears.

"There aren't any bears, you idiot." She muttered it to herself, but the sound carried and she clamped her mouth shut.

She hadn't survived this long by being stupid. And speaking in an unfamiliar environment when it was possible, if not probable, that there were untrustworthy people around wasn't smart.

Why was she so worried? Jaek wouldn't take her somewhere unsafe.

Unless he was about to betray her.

Her heartbeat kicked up and Carise decided she'd had enough. She could try and find the path and head back to Jaek's. He could explain why he'd walked away. Or she could run from him if he looked like he was in the process of betraying her. Maybe it would be smartest just to run and not give Jaek a chance to hurt her.

But she didn't think he would. Not when her body could still feel the impression of his lips against her.

She didn't know if she was making the right choice, but making *a* choice was better than standing still. Carise slung the bag over her shoulder and carried the blanket. With all their food gone, the bag wasn't particularly heavy, though she winced every time the cups clinked together. She hoped they didn't break.

She'd only made it to the very edge of the path when she froze. Her senses caught up to her instincts a second later and she heard voices.

"Can't be far," one man said.

"We're in the middle of the woods. We should go back and stake out the house before we get lost," said another man.

"He went back alone. Smart money is she's still out here. Do *you* want to fight that giant?" the first man asked.

Carise scrambled back, dropping the blanket and holding the bag as closely to her as she could, hoping the cups wouldn't clank. They didn't, but there weren't many places to hide.

Her first thought was to dive into the spring and swim behind the waterfall. But the water was not much more than a trickle and they'd see her quickly. All they'd have to do was fish her out of the water.

Or drown her.

Carise sprinted behind the rocks of the spring, hoping to find a path or a place to hide. She wanted to cry out for Jaek. The men coming for her seemed to think he was back at the cave, so she couldn't risk it. Not when it would give her position away.

How had they found her?

Had they followed them earlier? Had they *watched?*

Bile rose in her throat at the thought of her beautiful afternoon with Jaek being witnessed by strangers with dark intent. She put it out of her mind. She could cling to her memories later, but now she had to find a way to escape.

And she thought she had. A small path behind the spring was barely visible, but it looked like it went *somewhere*. Until she squeezed through and saw that her salvation was anything but.

There was no path. The trees were dense, twisted together as if they'd been weaved into fabric, and beside them was the rock of the spring, which climbed at least twice her height and left no footholds for her to attempt to scale it. She looked at the nearby tree, but she couldn't climb that either.

She was ready to squeeze back out when she heard something from outside.

"Someone was here!" one of the men yelled. "Look at this."

The blanket. She should have picked it back up, should have tried to erase any evidence of herself, but she hadn't even considered it as she ran.

It was too late to worry now.

Carise assessed her situation again. It wasn't the worst place to hide. If she got small and shrunk back into the shadows, they might not see her.

If she tried to get out, she feared they would.

She could hear them getting closer and shrank back against the rock, wishing for darker shadows but knowing she had nothing better. She looked at the trees again, but there was no way through, not with vines and bushes making a nasty wall on the ground.

Please don't see me.

It wasn't quite a prayer. She'd lost the taste for prayers after they'd gone unanswered for so long. She'd started pleading with the universe at some point. At least if the universe didn't answer her back, she couldn't get mad at God.

But she could use a miracle. Really.

Or Jaek.

If Carise let herself think of him, let herself worry, she'd despair. And she couldn't do that, not until all hope was lost. So she pushed thoughts of Jaek to the back of her mind. No thinking about him.

No thinking about *anything*. If she became one with the shadow, if she let herself drift into nothingness, maybe the men wouldn't see her.

She wasn't so lucky.

"Here, Baryn! I see her."

"Keep my name out of your mouth, you little shit." The other man, Baryn, snarled at the first man. She recognized that name. Was it the same man who'd dragged that human on a leash?

"Sorry, sir," he muttered. "But she's here. Hiding."

Carise held still as stone. She spied shadows moving on the other side of the trees she'd squeezed through. Maybe they were bluffing.

Were these Kru'dari as big as Jaek? She'd never be able to fight them.

"We see you," said Baryn. He stood just past the opening to her hidey-hole. "Now come out quietly and we won't harm you. Our boss wants to have a talk. Your sister was very persuasive."

The other man snorted. "She sure showed you."

"Shut up, Gav."

That made Carise stand up straighter. Her sister? Kenzie? She opened her mouth, tempted to ask, but clamped it closed again. It had to be a trick.

Though how would anyone know about Kenzie?

Unless Jaek had told them.

No. That she didn't believe. She wouldn't.

She kept her mouth shut and hoped they were bluffing, that they didn't really see her. But the men didn't go away.

"I can come in there," Baryn said conversationally. "But you won't like being alone with me. It's been a long day and I could use a break. You don't want to be my break."

She really didn't.

"Let's just cut her out of there," said Gav. He was eager. And younger, she was pretty sure. He wanted to impress. And people who wanted to impress were incredibly dangerous.

"Keep quiet," Baryn commanded. "Now, girl. It's your choice. You have one minute before I join you."

It felt like giving up. Carise had told Jaek she'd rather die than be taken again, but here under the threat of capture, she found out just how weak that resolve had been.

Because she didn't want to be alone with Baryn. She didn't want to find out what he would do to her when he got frustrated. If he tried to put a leash around her throat she would shatter into a billion pieces, never to recover.

She had no reason to trust he wouldn't hurt her the second he had his hands on her.

But he knew about Kenzie. And maybe her sister was in trouble.

Carise put the bag down as quietly as she could and hoped Baryn and Gav didn't notice. Maybe Jaek would find it. Maybe he would come for her.

"I'm coming out," she told Baryn. "I'm coming."

"Smart girl," he crooned, making her skin crawl.

She hoped Jaek was coming. Because she wouldn't survive again in captivity for long.

10

Jaek hated the thought of leaving Carise alone at the spring, but she'd loved it so much he'd had an idea they could camp there all night. They just needed more food and a warmer blanket.

She'd been sleeping so soundly he decided not to wake her up. He'd be gone for no more than an hour and she should be safe.

But every moment away from her was its own kind of torture.

Energy brimmed within him. Sex was usually almost as good as a fight when it came to generating the energy necessary for Kru'dari survival away from the Fount of Krudare. But this was *nothing* compared to a fight. He'd felt the way pure power had flowed into him while Carise gripped his hair as he feasted on her, and he felt like he could tear down a mountain with his bare hands.

Regular sex didn't do that.

A fight couldn't do that.

A mate could.

Fated mates were rare. Most mate bonds he'd seen on Guerran had nothing to do with fate. They were desperate connections made between Kru'dari starving for energy and hoping for scraps.

But a fated mate?

That was the strongest bond of all.

He'd suspected. Or perhaps hoped Carise might be his. He wanted to bind himself to her for good, their spirits intertwined so they could never be separated. But she couldn't know what that meant, and she'd already had her choices taken away.

And he was only *mostly* sure. It had been a long time since he'd last fucked. Maybe he was come-addled.

But he was almost certain it wasn't that. Almost certain that Carise was his.

He'd have to speak to her about it. Would she want him? Would she stay with him? Could Guerran be her home?

Jaek had never dreamed of a pardon. Krudare had been no great home to him, and he wouldn't miss it if it weren't for the Fount. The king wouldn't lower himself to pardon a single street thief.

But Jaek could leave.

Guerran didn't try to hold exiles. The exiles imprisoned themselves. To leave Guerran meant surrendering any possibility of a future pardon. If there was one law enforced on this forsaken planet it was that.

But there was a whole galaxy out there, one Carise might like to see. Would she want him at her side?

These were all questions for later. But they needed to talk. And he needed to make love to her again.

When he made it to the entrance of his cave, he was glad he'd come alone. The door was disturbed and someone was inside. Jaek balled his hands into fists, ready for a fight. He didn't like violence, but no one intruded on his home.

The air was tense as he stalked in. Mad was there, along with a human woman. "What the fuck are you doing here?" he demanded, the anger coming from fear that anyone else might have come to his place while Carise was there and defenseless. "And who's she?" He stared at the human woman for a moment and thought she looked familiar.

Had he seen her before?

The human scowled at him. "I'm—"

But Mad cut her off. "I'm helping Kenzie find her sister. She thinks she was dumped on Guerran in the last month or so. Do you know anything?"

Kenzie. He knew that name. But Mad was in his face and Jaek was angry. He didn't trust *anyone* with his Carise, not even Mad. "Haven't seen anyone." He shoved Mad aside. "Get out." Neither Mad nor Kenzie were eager to leave, no matter how hard Jaek glared. And if he wasn't willing to do more violence to his friend or his friend's woman, he'd have to deal with this. "I don't even know what this girl looks like," Jaek ground out. "Stop asking questions."

They needed to leave so he could get back to Carise. Everything would be alright once he was at her side again.

Kenzie stepped in front of him and tapped out a strange pattern on her arm before shoving it in his face. "How about now? Have you seen her?"

Words stopped in Jaek's throat. That was Carise, etched in ink on Kenzie's arm. Not quite the same woman he knew. The Carise of the tattoo looked happy, like she hadn't been dragged through all of the terrors that life had to offer.

His Carise had found her smile, but there were still shadows in her eyes. Shadows he wanted to chase away.

Kenzie backed up and Jaek had to force himself not to reach for her arm so he could study it. "I just want my sister back."

"That's enough." Mad stepped between them. "You don't need to touch her."

"This is my house." Jaek glared at Mad. "I can do what I want." Not that he wanted Kenzie.

But Kenzie wasn't going to put up with either him or Mad. "Have you seen Carise?" she demanded.

"Cari." He smiled. "Pretty name." Pretty woman. All his, waiting for him back at the spring. If only these two would go *away*.

Maybe Jaek should have told them. But he needed to

speak with Carise first. What if she decided she didn't want to be found?

"Not pretty." Kenzie glared at him. And if she knew what they'd done together earlier in the afternoon, she'd probably gut Jaek with one of her wicked looking knives. "My *sister*. Have you seen her?"

Jaek wanted another look at the tattoo, but it was already gone. "No," he lied.

Her glare edged toward a snarl. "If you hurt her, I'll end you."

Hurt her? Never. Jaek reeled at the suggestion. "Get out! Both of you!" He shoved at Mad. He wouldn't touch the human. Carise wouldn't like it if he hurt her sister.

Kenzie turned to Mad. "I think we're done here."

Mad froze where he stood, looking between her and Jaek. "Yeah, I think we are."

They walked out, and Jaek had the sinking feeling that something between them had irrevocably broken.

His thoughts of camping through the night dissolved in his need to get back and make sure Carise was safe. He rushed out of the cave, taking the necessary time to read-just his security measures, then he was sprinting back to the spring.

It was worry, nothing more. He'd arrive and she'd still be sleeping, with no idea that he'd gone. And then he'd tell her about her sister and matters would resolve themselves. He could discuss their potential mate bond with her later.

The first sign something was wrong was the blanket.

It was piled on the ground near the mouth of the trail, rather than laying beside the spring where it should have been.

Had Carise tried to walk back on her own?

He shouldn't have left her alone.

But he had to put those thoughts aside and find her. He didn't see the bag full of their belongings and he didn't see her.

"Carise?" Jaek called out. He didn't care about being heard by anyone else in the woods. He was the most dangerous thing for miles.

He didn't hear anything, not even the chirping of birds.

He searched around the spring, looking for signs of his woman. And it didn't take long to find footprints. Whoever had come here hadn't cared about covering their tracks.

Two of them. Kru'dari, given the size of their shoes.

They led behind the spring to a small break in the trees, a hidden little spot that might have made a perfectly romantic hideaway.

Or a trap.

He found the bag fallen on the ground beyond the trees, and saw that Carise's footsteps joined the two Kru'dari leading away.

They'd come for her and they'd taken her.

Jaek followed the footsteps, but they made their way down the same path he'd taken, and by the time they got near the city, the tracks were too faint to follow.

It didn't stop him. He tore his way through the city, demanding answers from anyone he passed. But either they hadn't seen anyone or they were too scared of what they had seen to answer. And that meant one thing.

The exile king. Jadirel. For some reason, his people had taken Carise. And getting her back could cost him everything.

Jaek didn't stop looking. One woman admitted to seeing Baryn and another man walking with an unhappy human. The woman had been wearing a dress covered in flowers, just like the one Carise had worn to the spring. They'd been walking towards Jadirel's palace.

But that was all he heard.

It took him all day, and night had long fallen by the time he admitted partial defeat.

He headed back to the cave and did what he should have done hours ago, if his anger hadn't been riding him so hard. He had security cameras set up outside. If they'd taken her from the spring, they might have passed right in front of his cave. He played the footage and it made his heart stop.

They'd been right in front of the cave. How had he missed them?

Carise looked toward it, and he could see in her eyes the second she decided *not* to call for help. Just as the woman in town had said, he recognized Baryn, and the other man was Gav, someone new to the planet and probably eager to gain favor. Carise tugged at the hold they had on her, trying to make a run for it.

But they were too big, too Kru'dari, for a small human to fight them.

Baryn slapped Carise.

Jaek reared back and yelled. He'd kill the man himself if he got his hands on him, but he needed to find him and Carise first.

He needed help.

He'd known he would pay for his lies, but he hadn't thought it would be so soon. At another time he might have hesitated, but he needed to find Carise and he knew of only one person who might be able to help.

The sister.

And he'd find the sister with Mad.

Mad's quarters were in the heart of Jadirel's territory. The streets were relatively quiet in the night, but that didn't mean no one was out. They were just staying clear of Jaek. Probably wise.

Jaek tromped up the stairs to Mad's door, and he unlocked it with a key Mad had given him long ago. The room was dark and Mad was a lonely lump on his bed. No sister.

Jake marched to the bathing chamber and threw open the door, but the room was empty. Mad had begun to stir, but Jaek didn't care that he'd woken Mad. This was too damn important.

"She's gone. Where is she?" he demanded. Mad sat up in his bed and put a knife on the side table. Clearly he hadn't realized Jaek was his intruder.

Or he'd been ready to stab Jaek. Was their friendship really so tarnished?

"I'm the only one here," Mad told him calmly.

Jaek didn't recognize the animalistic sound that came out of his throat and he slammed his hand against the wall, needing some sort of outlet. There was no telling what Carise was going through and he couldn't waste any more time.

"Are you saying you had Carise at some point?" Mad slid out of bed and made his way to the kitchen, where he started preparing tea, of all things. He flicked on a light so they could see.

Jaek could barely manage his words as he sunk into a chair and accepted a mug. "Cari's gone. Jadirel's men."

"Then why did you come here looking for her?" Mad sipped his own tea.

"Looking for the other one." Kenzie had crossed the galaxy looking for Carise, surely she could find her if they were on the same planet.

"I'm not sure where Kenzie is right now. We're meeting up again tomorrow. But I need to understand what happened. Why didn't you tell us you had Carise?" Mad kept asking his stupid questions, and Jaek wanted to throw his mug against the wall. They were wasting time.

"She's *mine*," Jaek ground out, every syllable daring Mad to contradict him. "Not letting her go."

"She's your mate?"

Jaek didn't have words for that. Was she? He hoped

she was with all his heart. But he couldn't say it. Not yet. Not when she was in such trouble. "I have to get her back."

"Calm down. Drink your tea." Mad glared at the mug until Jaek drank. "How long has Carise been with you? Are you bonded? Does she know about the connection? Does she trust you?"

"She trusts me," Jaek said. He wasn't going to bother with the rest of it. Trust was all that mattered. He'd promised to keep her safe and he'd failed.

Mad let it drop. "When was she taken?"

"A few hours ago." A few hours in the hands of torturers. She needed to get out of there. *He* needed to get her out.

"Do you know who took her?"

Now they were getting somewhere. "Baryn and that new kid he has working for him. Gav. I have security footage of them dragging her away." Desperation clawed at him. "She was struggling. She tried to fight. Baryn slapped her. I'll kill him."

Mad's voice grew dead serious. "You may need to get in line."

That confounded Jaek for a moment. "What?"

"Kenzie beat Baryn in the pit but didn't kill him." Mad grinned when he said it.

"Impossible. Cari said—" He cut himself off.

"I saw the fight with my own eyes."

Jaek stood up.

"Where are you going?" Mad glared at him, but Jaek wasn't cowed.

"To find Cari." They were getting nowhere. He needed to *move*.

Mad pointed at the seat. "Sit your ass back down. We're going to get her back. I promise. But that's not going to happen if you rush into Jadirel's palace without any backup. Now tell me, are you *sure* Baryn and Gav were working for Jadirel?"

Jaek nodded swiftly, still glaring at Mad for wasting his time.

Mad sucked in an unsteady breath. "Okay. I have a way into Jadirel's palace. We're going to get Carise back. You have my word."

"How?"

"Trust me."

Jaek was low on trust, but he nodded. They were going to get her back. It would all work out.

It had to.

11

It wasn't the first time Carise woke up in chains. It had to be the last. She could already feel the darkness of her former self encroaching on her, trying to make her smaller. And she feared that if she was here for long, there'd be nothing left of her.

She needed Jaek.

Would he come for her?

She hoped, but hope was the most dangerous emotion of them all. Hope broke a woman. And Carise had already been broken so many times she couldn't be put together anymore.

So she couldn't break again.

She shifted and the chains clinked.

"I know you're awake, dear girl." It was a man's voice, strangely soothing, like a kindly gentleman.

A liar's voice.

Carise opened her eyes and sat up. The more she

knew, the better. She was in a nice room, big, and beauti-fully decorated. Traitorously, her body realized the bed was even more comfortable than Jaek's.

But there were no windows. This was a pretty cell.

The man sitting in a chair at the foot of her bed was older, in his fifties if he'd been human. She didn't know how Kru'dari aged. He looked more like a politician than a warrior, and he wore a white tunic with delicate stitching details all along the shoulders.

This man was powerful. And he was playing a role. But what kind?

"I apologize for the chains, but they were quite necessary." He shifted back in his seat, resting his hands on his knees, a picture of cordial invitation.

Carise was surprised she had to bite back a quick retort. The man was probably a foot taller than her and outweighed her by a bit. Any Kru'dari could have subdued her.

Chains were overkill.

But she kept quiet. It was harder to screw up badly when you didn't say anything.

"You're quite coveted," the man continued. "Your sister Kenzie will be so happy to see you."

Carise jerked against her chains. "No!" She didn't mean to say it; she didn't want to give anything away. But how could Kenzie be stuck in this man's power? Was she chained up somewhere too? The questions lodged in the back of her throat.

And the man in the chair smiled. "So you *are* little Carise."

Carise stopped struggling and squeezed her eyes shut. How had this man read her so well? He must have realized she was unlikely to admit to her identity if he wanted to know it.

But now he did.

He stood. "I'll see that you have food in a bit. I have no intention of starving you or harming you beyond reason. If you don't make me. I can be a wonderful master. I think you might even come to love me."

She wanted to vomit.

The evil man didn't notice or care. "We shall speak more later. For now, I have things to do."

"Who *are* you?" It burst out of Carise. She wanted answers, and she wanted out, but the chains were heavy on her.

The man smiled even wider. "Jadirel, your king." He left.

She knew that name. It was the name of the man that Jaek was forced to work for. And now this man knew who her sister was. But how? And how did he know about Carise?

Could Kenzie really be on Guerran? Could she really see her sister again?

Carise didn't know what to hope. She couldn't let herself be used against her sister. She didn't want to be a pawn. And she knew Jadirel was dangerous.

But how could she get out?

She tugged again on the chains, but they didn't budge. And Carise hadn't suddenly developed super strength or the ability to pick locks. She was going to be a pawn no matter what.

She collapsed back onto the bed and tears came. Everything had been so perfect that morning. How could it have gone so wrong?

A while later someone brought her a tray of food, but Carise didn't eat it. She didn't want to be drugged. Though maybe Jadirel wouldn't bother.

Every so often she tugged at the chain, but it never slackened. And after a while, she gave in to sleep. It was fitful, but it happened.

She had no idea how much time had passed. The lack of windows was screwing with her. Eventually she found out she could reach a small bathroom right beside the bed, as the chain was designed to stretch that far.

She had enough chain to kill herself.

She was staring at the metal and contemplating that fate for a long time. She didn't want to die. Not when things had just started with Jaek. Not when Kenzie might be so close to finding her.

But she didn't want to be *used*.

She also didn't want to die.

Carise put the thought out of her mind. For now. She wasn't going to do it until things turned *really* dire. Of course, by then it might already be too late.

There was a commotion outside the door. What would it be now? Torture? Experiments? Worse?

It died down after a while. Had hours passed? Days? She'd slept once and been given food once. No one had come to take it away, and she eyed it hungrily. She wasn't the hunger strike type, and if they fed her again, she'd eat it.

But not yet. She wasn't giving in.

There was more commotion. A few minutes later, the lock in the door clicked and a guard walked inside.

"Hold out your hands," he said. "I'm to deliver you to the queen."

Carise didn't hold out her hands. She scampered back. The king was bad enough. What would his queen be like?

"What's going on?" she demanded with more bravery than she felt. "What's happened?"

The guard waved the key at her. "You'll find out. If you let me take you to the queen. She demanded to see you at once. First act."

First act? Was that some saying on Guerran that Carise was supposed to understand? Curiosity overcame her fear. She held out her hands and let the guard unchain her.

He noticed the untouched plate of food. "Not hungry?" he asked. "Did you want something else?"

He didn't put her in different chains as he led her out the door. People rushed to and fro in the hallway, and in the chaos, Carise could probably make a run for it. But she was even more interested now. "Do you really care what I want?"

"Yes, of course." The guard was too accommodating. Nothing like the king.

What the ever loving hell?

The walk down the hall was long, and Carise's stomach started grumbling halfway there. Maybe this queen, whoever she was, would feed her. She really regretted ignoring the meal.

Too late now.

The hallways were wider here, and the activity even more frenzied. Something big had happened. And all while Carise was chained up in another room. She hated to miss out on the excitement.

She snorted. No. She'd had more than enough excitement to last three lifetimes. She just wanted to curl up next to Jaek and live a simple life.

And find Kenzie. Or get word to her. Jadirel thought she was on Guerran, so it could happen. Once she figured out what was going on. But Carise was starting to hope. Everything felt strange right now, and when things got weird, anything was possible.

The guard pushed open the door.

And her big sister was standing right there, a shocked grin on her face.

12

KENZIE CLUTCHED HER IN A HUG, and tears threatened to spill down Carise's cheeks. She didn't know what to say. Words caught in her throat. She'd really never expected to see Kenzie again, no matter what she'd hoped.

And here she was.

Somehow Kenzie was a *queen* on Guerran. There was a whisper behind her about *clearing away the body*, but Carise was too busy focusing on Kenzie to catch who was dead.

Jadirel? Hopefully she could get Kenzie to explain.

"You're taller!" Kenzie exclaimed as she pulled back.

Carise smiled faintly. "It happened after Earth. Space supplements or something." She wasn't going to go into detail about all of the horrible things that had been done to her. She often forgot she was supposed to be a bit shorter.

They settled onto a small couch, Carise scrunching

up into a ball and pulling her legs close. Kenzie took up so much *space*. She was somehow *more* than Carise remembered, her personality taking up half the room even though she was only a normal human woman.

"How long have you been on Guerran?" Kenzie asked.

Time was hard to think about. It all flew by, and Carise had no idea how long she'd been held captive on Guerran before she found Jaek. So she said the first thing that popped into her mind. "About a month, I think." Was that right? Could it be?

It didn't matter. The past was the past.

Kenzie accepted that, so Carise couldn't be that far off. And then she asked something that made Carise's heart pound. "What's up with Jaek?"

Kenzie knew Jaek? How? Kenzie was in defensive older sister mode, and if Carise admitted half the things they'd done together, her sister would probably do unpleasant things to him. So she kept it simple. And true. "He was nice. He kept me safe."

Kenzie didn't seem to know how to process that. "He's... um... big."

Carise blushed and hid her face behind her knees. Her sister had *no* idea. "They're all big here." But that wasn't the important part now. "How did you do this? How are you here? Am I dreaming?" They were on the other side of the galaxy from Earth, so many light years away that the journey should have been impossible. And yet they were sitting next to one another on a couch in a palace on Guerran.

"I'm really here," Kenzie assured her, reaching out and clutching her hand to anchor her in the moment. "I made a lot of contacts back on EarthCol3, and I called in every favor. I haven't stopped looking since I found out you were gone. Then I got here and I found you." She didn't give Carise a second to process that before she kept talking. "It shouldn't be too difficult to get passage off of Guerran. We're a long way from Earth. But we can probably be home for Christmas. I think. I'm not actually sure what month it is back home. But if we missed it, we can have our own."

"Don't tell me you're going to make fruitcake," Carise moaned, her face a mass of exaggerated horror while her mind reeled. *Earth?* Did she really want to go back? Was Kenzie going to even ask what she wanted to do?

Where was Jaek? *What* was going on?

Kenzie didn't see Carise's growing distress. She was too busy smiling. "I will make fruitcake and you're going to like it. No matter how burned it is. Or we could do cookies. Ham. Mashed potatoes. Mac and cheese. Whatever you want, we'll have."

"What—" Carise cut herself off. What would Kenzie say if she said she didn't want to go home yet?

That wasn't the unspoken question her sister heard. She was too busy imagining what Carise wanted to pause and see if she was right. "We don't have to do Christmas," Kenzie was quick to say. "Right, what am I thinking. If I had found you sooner—"

"What? No!" Carise interrupted. Her frustration

dissolved into smoke for the moment. She wouldn't let Kenzie blame herself for everything. "You crossed the galaxy to find me, that's practically impossible. And you did it in two years!" She gripped her sister's hands.

But Kenzie was fierce and insistent. "You should have never been taken in the first place. If I hadn't abandoned you at home, you would have been safe. And when we get back, you don't have to worry. No matter what. You're not getting taken again."

Carise was quiet for a moment, and then she smiled. "I would like ham. And pie." And maybe they could get them on Guerran. She just had to work up the courage to say what she wanted. Why couldn't she speak?

"Consider it done."

They talked for at least an hour before a hulking Kru'-dari man who looked at Kenzie with hearts in his eyes told them a room had been made up for Carise. No one told her who that guy was.

Seriously. What the hell was going on?

"You should sleep," Kenzie told her as they followed a servant down the winding hallways to a new room with a window that overlooked a courtyard and a blazing fire in the fireplace.

"I'm not tired," Carise insisted, even as she sat on the bed. She opened her mouth to ask what was going on, but her stomach grumbled loud enough for them both to hear.

"Food then?" Kenzie grinned.

Carise nodded. Food and an explanation would be good.

Kenzie stepped out of the room for a few minutes and came back with a tray laden with goodies. A servant followed behind her with two glasses of wine. "No pie. Sorry."

Carise took the wine she was offered and sipped, enjoying the dry taste. Of course, there was a risk of it going to her head with her empty stomach. Too bad. "You don't have to keep apologizing for everything. It's not your fault. I can wait for my goddamn pie."

She wanted Kenzie to smile, to laugh. But she looked at Carise like she'd grown a second head. They had a long way to go before their sisterly bond was healed. "Drink up," she said, watching Carise intently.

Carise drank, and picked at the food. Every time she tried to ask what was going on, Kenzie spoke over her, making plans to return to Earth and get Carise the "healing help" she needed.

She didn't explain what was going on in this palace or why she seemed to have power. She didn't explain who that huge Kru'dari man was. She didn't say another word about Jaek.

Did she think Carise couldn't handle the truth?

Or was there more going on that Carise didn't understand?

She wanted to be happy that Kenzie had found her. She was, she *really* was. But she couldn't help but feel frustrated, too. And before long, Carise started yawning. The wine seemed to knock her out.

She curled up on the bed and slowly surrendered to sleep. She'd get answers in the morning, she promised herself. Everything would make sense then. But right then, she couldn't keep her eyes open for another moment.

She hoped all made sense when she woke up.

13

Jaek waited for the signal. Then he waited some more. *He* should be the one storming Jadirel's palace and rescuing Carise. He knew that to the depths of his soul. And yet he'd been forced to leave it to Mad.

And he'd been forced to stay behind. If Mad failed in his challenge of the king, then it would be up to Jaek to try on his own.

Hours had gone by and night had fallen. He should have heard something by now. He was tired of waiting. He grabbed a club, just in case he needed a weapon, and marched through the city.

The first sign something was different was when he wasn't challenged for entry into Jadirel's palace. The place was in an uproar and he slipped inside like it was nothing.

He found Mad and his human in the throne room. Jadirel was nowhere to be seen.

That meant only one thing. He was dead. And Carise was safe. And Mad was an exile king.

"Where is she?" he demanded. He needed to see Carise, to make sure she hadn't been harmed. He didn't know how Mad and the human could be standing there like nothing was wrong. Had they even *seen* Carise?

Kenzie muttered something that Jaek couldn't quite make out. She pulled out of her embrace with Mad and turned to Jaek. "She's sleeping," she said. "And she's okay. Thank you for taking care of her." She choked on those last words.

"I want to see her." Jaek stomped further into the room, and his grip tightened on his club. He was ready to bust heads, but all the heads had been busted. If he could just see Carise, just prove to himself that she was safe, all would be well.

Was that so much to ask?

"You can't," Mad said. He stepped half a step in front of Kenzie, blocking Jaek from going any further. "Come in the morning. Or stay here tonight and see her in the morning. Either is acceptable. But Carise needs her sleep."

Anger pounded in his veins, all of it piling on top of itself until it roared itself to unending life. He'd waited. He'd been patient. He'd let his *friend* take the privilege of saving Carise.

And now Mad thought he could keep Jaek away from her?

He jabbed his club at Mad, but he wasn't crazy

enough to actually hit the man. "I want to see her now," he demanded. "I won't wake her up." Rather than wait for permission, he charged forward.

The sister stepped between him and the hallway. Did she never stop interfering? "Not going to happen today."

Something glinted in the light. The human had a knife. Jaek's anger overflowed. He let out a bellow and charged her before she could use the knife to harm him. Mad surged in front of him and tackled Jaek to the floor, landing a harsh blow on his face.

Mad got to his feet and glared down at Jaek. "Get out."

Jaek raised his fingers to his eye, realizing what he'd done. How had he lost control like that? "Mad—"

"You tried to hurt my mate." He leaned in close and Jaek expected another blow. But Mad only scowled. "Get out of my territory until you learn some manners."

Jaek wanted to apologize. He wanted to stay and talk and say this was all one big misunderstanding. Instead he got to his feet, scooped up his club, made a rude gesture at the new exile king, and walked out muttering curses.

He couldn't trust Mad now. No exile king could be trusted. They were the law, such as it was, on Guerran, and they took cruel pleasure in taking everything out on the people in their territory.

Mad's not like that.

Jaek shoved the thought aside. Mad didn't even remember that it was *Jaek* who'd brought him information about Carise. He couldn't take the slightest bit of pity on him and allow Jaek to just look at her. Was that so much to ask?

He meant to go home, but he ended up detouring to The White Flower, a small restaurant that was open at all hours and a hub of activity. He'd hired informants there before and conducted business, but not for years.

And it wasn't his domain any longer.

A human woman was one of the only people in the room when he entered. She sat at a table in the back corner and observed him with assessing eyes.

Layala.

She'd arrived on Guerran several years before with no past and no money, but she'd carved a place for herself. And now she sat at the heart of one of the strongest information networks on the planet. Even the exile kings were scared of her.

Jaek wasn't supposed to know that.

A spymaster didn't survive for long if everyone knew who she was. But Jaek had his own eyes and ears throughout Orion, and he knew enough.

Layala nodded to the chair opposite her. "Sounds like there was some excitement tonight."

"You have a part of that?" He might have known what she did, but her ends were still a mystery. This was the most stupid place he could have ended up tonight. He didn't need to speak to Layala.

And yet, he happily accepted an ale when the server put it in front of him.

"I can't say I'm disappointed the old man is dead. Or that I thought Mad had it in him. That boy is too honorable for Guerran. I'm surprised he's lasted this long." She poured herself a mug of tea from a teapot. "Did they find the girl?"

Jaek's hand froze on his glass, and it was as good as an admission. Layala read people far too well. And he needed to say *something*. Maybe the spymaster would understand.

Or maybe Jaek was a fool.

"She was safe with me until that human showed up. Jadirel didn't give a shit. And the second I find out the sister is looking for her, his men come by and snatch her up. She'll be gone soon and I'll never even..." He choked down his ale rather than speak his fears.

But that had to be what the sister wanted. Why would anyone stay on Guerran when they didn't have to?

Layala's eyebrows rose a fraction. "You think Kenzie will leave? Even though she's developed a liking for the new exile king?"

"He called her his mate." Jaek felt a sharp stab of satisfaction at delivering the information, especially when it was clear that Layala hadn't known.

"So he'll leave with her, if she leaves."

Jaek shrugged. No way to know. He sipped his ale.

Layala drank her tea. They sat in silence for several moments, until Layala finally spoke again. "I'm curious to see where Mad's rule goes. I don't want him gone. I think he could actually do some good on this terrible rock."

Jaek agreed. Even at his most angry with his friend, he knew Mad wasn't a monster. "They've got what they want," was all he said.

"Yes." She nodded at him. "Finish your ale and begone. I have work to do. And you'll regret being seen here in the morning, we both know it."

Jaek finished the drink. "Hurt Carise and I'll end you."

Layala rolled her eyes. "Begone, giant. Your little human will come to no harm."

He wanted to ask her what she was planning. He wanted to tell her to stop. Or to let him help. He should have never spoken to her in the first place. But what was done was done, and nothing could stop a determined Layala.

Jaek left and hoped he wasn't making a huge mistake.

———

Carise woke with a pounding head and an ugly tasting mouth. One glass of wine shouldn't have done that.

Had she been drugged?

No. Of course not. Kenzie wouldn't—

Kenzie!

She shot up and winced at the pain in her head. And

when she did so, she shifted the pillow she'd slept on to reveal a note.

Your sister plans to take you off this planet today. Visit me if you are not ready to leave. You have Jaek's guarantee of your safety.

Tell her something to keep her from following you.

- A Friend

Carise stared at the note for a long time, not quite sure she understood what it said. She had no idea who'd written it, no reason to believe it. There were additional instructions about how to get out of the palace and where to go.

It could so easily be a trap.

But someone had put it in her room. Who?

She should show it to Kenzie. That was the smart move. She had a lot of questions for her sister, and she could start with who was delivering mysterious notes while she slept.

But if Kenzie thought she was in danger, she'd be even more eager to leave.

The note was a lie. It had to be.

And yet, it held the ring of truth. Kenzie had barely let her talk the night before while she laid out their plans. She *was* determined to get Carise off Guerran.

And Carise needed to see Jaek again.

She couldn't leave Guerran. She couldn't let Kenzie take control like she always did and bundle Carise up until the safety she was being provided felt like a prison. She'd been growing these last weeks with Jaek, finding herself again and beginning to feel, well, not safe. Never safe on Guerran. But she was beginning to feel like herself again.

Not the old Carise. That girl was gone. But she could figure out who the new, free, Carise was.

And Kenzie wouldn't want that. She'd want the old Carise back and she'd be disappointed when Carise couldn't be that person.

Carise couldn't just blithely slide back into Kenzie's life. It was tempting. Oh, so tempting.

But she needed her freedom.

She studied the note again. It wasn't from Jaek. But whoever wrote it knew about Jaek.

So had the bad guy who'd abducted her.

Two weeks ago, Carise wouldn't have been able to even *consider* walking away from the safety her sister offered.

Now she needed to. She couldn't accept anyone's cage, not even Kenzie's.

There was a small desk near her bed. She pulled out paper and a pen and started writing. The words came so naturally they must have been pent up all night.

Dear Kenzie,

I'm sorry for leaving like this. I'm safe and with a friend. I know that's not going to stop you worrying about me, so I promise that I will send a note to check in at least once a week.

Thank you so much for coming for me. I knew you would. Even in the darkest days, I knew my big sister would come. That hope kept me alive when nothing else would. And you came! You freed me! I was so happy to see you and I love you so much.

But I need to figure things out for me. You were making so many plans last night that I didn't have time to get a word in edgewise. I don't want to go back to Earth, at least not yet. And it's not about Jaek, I promise. He ALSO kept me safe for a little while, but that's not it.

This is about me.

For the first time in years, I have my freedom. I want to figure out who I am and what I want. And I'm afraid that if I leave here with you, I'm not going to be able to do that. You're a little overprotective, okay?

I'm a big girl now. Let me figure out how to take care of myself.

This isn't goodbye AT ALL. We're going to see each other again and we're going to be sisters. But I need my time. Please give it to me.

I will always love you. I will always be your little sister.

But let me figure out who I am now.

-Carise

She looked down at the words and they all felt true. She needed to do this.

Carise dressed quickly and left, following the instructions and hoping she wasn't making a mistake.

She ended up at a small restaurant and found a human woman sitting at a table in the front of the room. "You got my note."

The woman claimed she knew Kenzie and introduced

herself as Layala. Carise didn't see Jaek anywhere, and she tried not to be disappointed. She'd find him.

Eventually.

"I'm glad you came to see me," Layala said, as if she hadn't dangled the bait in front of Carise.

"Why?" She was weary, but curious. Layala didn't seem eager to hurt her. Maybe this hadn't been a stupid decision after all.

"I'd like to offer you a job."

14

Three Weeks Later

Carise dropped off her latest note to Kenzie with one of the runners before checking in to see if she had any more errands to run in her quadrant. Layala hadn't been lying about the job. It was real work, for real money, with real protection.

For the first time in years, Carise was acting for herself. There was no master, no chains. No guards.

No Kenzie.

No Jaek.

She'd wanted to go running off to Jaek the same day she'd met Layala. And her boss wouldn't have stopped her. But it was dangerous to cross the city, and Carise had been afraid. And she hadn't wanted to ask Layala for an escort.

Nor did she want to go back to Kenzie. Layala had

explained what happened that night, even though Kenzie should have been the one to do it.

Carise had been abducted by the former exile king's men. Mad had challenged the king, Jadirel, in single combat, and he'd won. Mad was Kenzie's mate, and so she now stood as queen beside him.

And they'd done it all to free Carise.

It made Carise feel *a little* bad for running away. But that feeling faded the longer she stayed away.

Her feelings for Jaek didn't. She hadn't been brave enough to send a note to him. For some reason she was almost afraid of what would happen if she saw him again. Would he carry her back to his cave and keep her there? Would he drag her back to Kenzie?

Would he let her make her own path?

Jaek had been so careful and protective with her. And his kisses had made her burn. But she couldn't be dependent on anyone if she wanted real freedom.

Carise checked in at the restaurant and Layala was sitting at her table, drinking tea alone.

"Sit," her boss told her. "Have you eaten?"

Carise shook her head, and Layala flagged down someone to bring out a meal. Carise accepted it gratefully. Layala was generous with food and drink, and half the time it meant that Carise didn't have to waste her credits on food.

"How is the roommate working out?" Layala asked while Carise finished off her meal.

Carise chewed and swallowed. "Good, good. She's…" She stumbled over what she should say.

"Always busy?" Layala suggested. "I thought you might like someone who gave you your personal space."

Carise wasn't sure about that, but having some space to herself wasn't a bad thing, at least. Her roommate also worked for Layala, but Carise wasn't sure what she did. She wasn't sure what Layala did, exactly, but it involved a lot of employees and a lot of errands.

Carise didn't need to know more. Yet.

Layala flicked her fingers in the air and one of the wait staff brought her a package. "I need you to deliver this package to this address," she said, sliding a card across the table. "You will meet a Kru'dari named Fynn. He's… charming." Disdain dripped with the words. "Hand this over and if he has any messages, report back directly. This is a sensitive matter."

Carise took the package. "Got it."

Layala held up a hand to keep her from leaving. "Dump the package and forget the name if anyone stops you."

Carise nodded. "Of course. I'll see you later."

"Safe travels."

Carise left the restaurant with her bag slung over her shoulder, the package safely inside. It was a bit more cloak and dagger than usual. For her first week she hadn't done anything by herself, instead trailing after Layala's errand runners and learning the ropes.

The second week she'd worked in the kitchen, but it

had quickly become clear that she wasn't a very good cook or waitress. But errands? She could run errands and messages with the best of them.

The streets of Orion weren't as scary as they had once been, even if she was certain she could feel eyes watching her every so often. But now she had a small blast stick to use if anyone tried anything. It carried a charge that could incapacitate three Kru'dari at once and reminded her just a bit of a cattle prod.

She hadn't had to use it. People knew she worked for Layala, and Layala's people were protected.

She waved at a few of the shop owners who she'd gotten to know and felt like she was really making a home here. It wasn't Earth. It was barely civilized. She was surrounded by convicted criminals every moment of every day.

And yet she felt free.

Carise quickly found the address Layala had sent her to. The place wasn't much better than a hovel, with a half-collapsed roof and rotting drapes in front of the windows. But Fynn, whoever he was, warranted a personal courier from Layala, so clearly the terrible accommodations weren't the entire story.

She would have knocked, but the door was already swinging on its hinge and she feared it would fall off if she hit it too hard. When she gave it a tiny push, it swung open. Carise stepped inside. The place smelled dusty, but not too dirty. It could have been worse. There were a few pieces of old wooden furniture and a nest of blankets in one corner that might have been a bed.

"Hello!" she called out. "Is anyone here?" She didn't move far from the door. If this Fynn person turned out to be bad news, she wanted to be able to run. The package felt heavy in her hands. Under other circumstances, she might have just left it, but she had instructions.

There was a noise through a half-hidden doorway at the back of the room and a shadow fell across the opening. Carise's breath caught for a moment, blood fizzing with the need to run. But she held her ground. She was here to do her job, not turn into a coward.

A Kru'dari wearing a soft looking robe, his hair short and slicked back, walked into the room. He was nearly as tall as Jaek. Nearly as hot too, with a wide smile on his face and trouble in his eyes.

"Well hello," he said. He didn't sound like Jaek. His voice was more clipped. Jaek had a tendency to fudge his vowels and drop letters off of words, as if he couldn't be bothered to do more than mumble. "I must have done something right for the pleasure of your company."

This guy talked like he was rich.

It was hard to tell with communicators sometimes—they could power over accents and through nuances of speech—but there was something about the way this man talked that made her think money.

And if he was rich, he must have done something really bad to end up on Guerran. At least, that was if

Kru'dari justice was anything like what she'd expect back home.

"What's your name?" Carise asked. The man was attractive, but no one she wanted. She had eyes for exactly one man, even if she was *trying* to put him out of her mind while she figured herself out.

The man stepped farther into the room. "I'd think you'd know that since you found me. Or have you stumbled into my little cave, all innocent and in need of a protector?"

"This isn't a cave." She shouldn't take the bait, but there was one cave she wanted to see above all others.

But she couldn't rely on Jaek until she was sure she could rely on herself. That was the whole point of this experiment.

The man waved a hand, as if swatting away her point. "Yes, yes. Tell me who you're looking for, and I'll let you know if I am he."

"Tell me who you are and I'll tell you if you're right." Layala wanted her couriers to be careful about who they handed packages off to. She couldn't give this man Fynn's name, otherwise he might lie and take the package off her hands. And while she didn't think Layala would beat her for screwing up, Carise didn't want to find out.

"A name is a heavy thing to give away," said the man.

She was getting sick of this. "Listen, sir, I just need your name. If you're who you're supposed to be, a mutual friend has something for you. So what's your name?"

That caused him to straighten, and the smile disappeared from his face as he was suddenly all business. "Layala sent it?" he demanded.

"I don't know. What's your name?" Really, this was getting frustrating.

The man blew out a breath. "She would call me Fynn. Now hand it over."

That was what she needed. Carise held out the package and the man, Fynn, snatched it from her hands. She was kind of curious to see what it was and didn't immediately turn around and leave. Fynn noticed her hesitation and glanced up at her.

"Did you want to stick around for a tumble? The package can wait." He grinned.

"I need to get back. Goodbye." She fled. The old Carise, the one from Earth, might have managed to flirt with that guy. She used to like flirting. It could mean nothing or everything, and it kept her mind sharp.

But flirting felt like a betrayal.

It was stupid. She'd been apart from Jaek now longer than she'd been with him. But none of her feelings had faded. They should have. Right? It wasn't like he'd come for her. She wasn't hiding. If he tried, he'd find her.

Carise snapped her gaze behind her as her neck prickled with awareness.

No one was there. She wasn't being followed. It was just hyper-vigilance. She'd get over it.

She checked in at the restaurant to let Layala know the package was successfully delivered and started home. It had been a long day and she was ready to collapse into bed.

But it still felt like someone was watching her.

She sped up, wishing her little rooms were closer to the restaurant. She glanced down the narrow alley she'd normally take and faltered. The shadows were long and anyone could be hiding. If she went around the block instead, it would take ten more minutes, but it wouldn't feel so claustrophobic.

"You're panicking over nothing," she told herself. This had happened a couple of times before, these little fits. Leftover treats from her time in captivity. And she wasn't going to let them control her.

Carise turned towards the alley and took a steadying breath. Her hands trembled every step she took, but she made it through.

The alley wasn't the problem. It was the exiles waiting on the other side. Three of them, all with leers on their faces that made her want to run the other way.

One grabbed for her.

Carise hit him. It didn't do much. She was still so much smaller compared to all of these aliens. But she hit again, stomping on one of the exiles' feet.

"You're coming with us," one of them said. "We have unfinished business."

"I don't know who you are," she replied, as if she

could make them believe this was all some misunderstanding.

"Ba—"

"Hey! Let her go," someone called from in the alley.

She knew that voice. She'd feared she'd never hear
that voice again.

Jaek stalked closer, and his words took on a more
sinister tone as the three men didn't back up. "I said let
her go."

15

FOR THREE WEEKS, Jaek had suffered in agony knowing his mate was out there and that he couldn't touch her. All he'd wanted was to gather her close and take her home with him where he could keep her safe forever.

Instead he'd watched from afar as she found her footing working for Layala. And as the days went on, she didn't come for him. He wouldn't force her.

But he could watch over her.

And today he was glad he did. He didn't recognize the three exiles who'd cornered her, but that didn't matter. He stepped between Carise and the one closest to her, and got close to his face.

"One warning," he said, voice dripping with menace. "I will let you walk away. Now go."

He gave them a chance, but there was an eagerness for a fight brewing on the three men's faces. Jaek still hated fighting. But he would gladly make these exiles bleed if it meant keeping Carise safe.

He counted to ten in his head, but didn't tell them to walk again. They knew the terms. And he hadn't survived so long on Guerran without building a reputation for himself.

At seven, one of the men broke and fled. Jaek was big, and he could be brutal. And everyone knew it.

The other two men didn't care.

"We just want the girl," the man he'd warned said. "No need to fight. We can share."

Carise made a choked sound, and all Jaek wanted to do was gather her into his arms and tell her all would be well.

And it would. Once he'd removed all of the teeth from these two exiles' mouths. "Say that again," he dared.

"We're not supposed to—" the second man tried to speak.

The first cut him off. "Shut it. We're taking the girl."

Enough was enough. Jaek punched him and he went down. It was a lucky hit to the jaw. If the exile had seen it coming, it never would have worked. But Jaek wasn't here for a long, drawn out battle.

He wanted it done.

The second exile was smarter. He dodged back when Jaek hit and got in a few shots of his own. But he wasn't particularly skilled or fast, and Jaek had speed and fury on his side.

Once he got the first hit in, it was over. His victim just didn't know it yet. Blood coated Jaek's fists and it wasn't his own. His opponent spat out a broken tooth and Jaek felt a sick sense of satisfaction as a dark cloud of hate settled over him. Energy from the fight swirled around them and Jaek sucked it up hungrily, his spirit open to it even as he felt sick in feeding off another. But with no access to the Fount, there was little choice.

He was going to finish this.

But before he could get in another punch, the man he was fighting turned on his heel and sprinted away.

Jaek almost chased. He almost hunted him down and beat him to a pulp. But he forced himself to stop.

Carise.

She was his reason. She was the one in trouble. He had to protect his mate.

He stepped over the body of the fallen man, who was already starting to groan and stir. If he was smart, he'd run away before Jaek came back.

But where was Carise?

She was supposed to be standing there, but she wasn't. Had someone grabbed her while he'd been distracted with the fight? Fury roared through him at the thought, and he would make whoever it was pay.

But that wasn't it.

He heard a hiccuping cry come from the alley, and it pulled Jaek's heart out of his chest. He knew those tears.

Carise had fitted herself behind a pile of debris next to the cracked brick of one of the buildings, hiding from sight, her arms wrapped around her midsection and her face a mask of terror.

Jaek stepped closer and she flinched.

He froze.

He looked at his hands and saw his knuckles were cracked and covered in another man's blood. He wiped them as best he could against his shirt, hiding as much of the evidence as he could. But Carise still shrank back from him.

It stabbed him in the heart, and he could feel protestations try and rise in his throat. But he knew this wasn't about him. His Carise had suffered so much, she'd been so strong. Of course something would crack her shields.

Everyone broke. Eventually.

Jaek sank to his knees and reached for her. And this time, she didn't flinch from him. She let him wrap his arms around her hips and pull her close, his body a silent shield, a promise that no more harm could come to her.

He'd failed her so many times already. Once when Jadirel's men came for her. Again when he couldn't see her when Mad became exile king. And now, letting those men terrorize her.

No more.

He stroked his fingers over her side. She'd gained a little more weight, no longer the bony, fragile woman he'd first rescued. She stood taller, even when she was terrified, and eventually her arms came around and rested on his shoulders, holding him to her.

"It's okay," he promised. He wanted to tell her that

she'd never be threatened again, that he wouldn't let it happen.

But this was Guerran, and he didn't want to lie to her.

He didn't know how long they were like that, her huddled against the wall, him kneeling in front of her, but eventually they stopped. Carise tugged him up and wrapped her arms around him, plastering herself to his front.

He'd suffer exile a hundred times to be in her arms like this. He'd refuse a pardon and damn the king, so long as he got to keep her.

"Come on," Jaek said after a while. The alley was starting to stink and he didn't want to attract any more opportunists. "Let me take you home."

Carise smiled up at him and nodded. "I missed you," she said.

He didn't know what it meant to miss a person until she was taken from his life. And though it was probably the last thing he should do while the vestiges of terror still clung to her and he was still partially covered in other men's blood, he leaned down and captured her lips with his own.

Carise curled her fingers into his shirt and kept him close, opening her mouth and tangling her tongue with his in a desperate motion of need. His lust roared to life and he almost had her right there in the alley, against the wall for any to see.

He forced himself to pull away, breathing heavily and wanting nothing more than to kiss her forever.

Her eyes were dark with lust, her breaths heavy. He could make out the outline of her breasts under her tunic, the swell of her hips. Her body was a delight he wanted to explore again and again.

He needed to send her home, needed to let her make any irrevocable choice with plenty of time to think. He knew that if he got her alone, there was no turning back. She was his mate, even if she didn't know it, and his soul needed her more than he needed the energy of the Fount.

"Take me home, Jaek," Carise commanded. Her voice didn't tremble and her gaze was clear. She knew what she was asking.

And he was helpless to resist.

16

THEY DIDN'T SPEAK MUCH on the walk back to Jaek's, and once they were safely inside, he left her alone for a few moments to wash off the evidence of his fight with the other men.

With someone else, Carise might have been nervous. They both knew why there were there. They both knew where this night was going. But instead of nerves, she was just impatient for Jaek to come out from the bathroom and join her again.

How long did it take for a man to wash his hands?

Frenetic energy welled up within her until she had to start pacing or go crazy. Somehow Jaek's cave was bigger than she remembered. Or maybe it was just that her new apartment was tiny in comparison.

And this place felt more like home than any other place she'd lived.

That counted her home back on Earth.

She'd only stayed there a couple of weeks, at most. She still wasn't sure of the exact stretch of time.

And yet.

The water cut off and Carise watched the bathroom door like her life depended on it. A minute passed, and then another. And Jaek still didn't come out.

Was he stalling? Had he changed his mind? Was she the only one who'd been living in agony these past weeks hoping he would come to her, even as she desperately clung to her newfound independence?

She was supposed to be figuring out life on her own, not falling into Jaek's bed like she'd never left.

But no number of vicious exiles could drag her out of Jaek's quarters. Not now that she was finally back where she belonged.

The bathroom door opened and Carise's breath caught. No, Jaek wasn't walking away.

He'd stripped out of his clothes and wore only the soft robe she'd claimed as her own while she lived with him. It was belted loosely, revealing his broad chest and the hair she wanted to run her fingers through. All he had to do was untie the belt and he'd be as good as naked.

And now she felt overdressed.

"Carise..." Her name tore out of him like a prayer and she shivered.

"Jaek." She didn't recognize the sound of her own voice, low and desperate and a bit breathy. She was hot with need, empty and waiting, nearly trembling with the force it took to keep from throwing herself at her huge alien.

Jaek reached out but pulled his hand quickly back before she could touch him. "We should talk," he said. He sounded anguished.

Again, Carise was afraid he'd changed his mind.

"You hate talking." She stepped close and put her hand on his chest, her fingers tangling in his chest hair and heated by the warm skin underneath. He was strung tight and ready to snap. She didn't know what was holding him back or why. "Kiss me now and we'll talk later." She couldn't keep track of a conversation now if she tried.

With a groan, Jaek gave into the passion swirling between them. He picked her up as if she weighed nothing and Carise wrapped her legs around his waist, his robe doing nothing to hide his growing arousal. He kissed her fiercely and Carise surrendered to it.

What more could she do when it was the only thing she wanted in the world?

He didn't stop kissing her as he stepped his way to the bed and set her down, coming down on top of her and covering her body with his own. Somehow instead of feeling caged in, she felt protected, and she clung to Jaek, fearful that if he pulled back, everything between them might stop.

How could it stop? She wanted this to last forever.

But her clothes were in the way. Stupid fabric.

Jaek's hand teased under her shirt until he cupped a

breast, his thumb brushing over one of her nipples. Carise moaned into his lips, her body arching up into him. And when he pinched, bringing her just to the line between pleasure and pain, Carise nearly exploded, her heartbeat pounding and her body on fire.

"Too much?" Jaek pulled back, face a mask of concern, his eyes dark with lust.

"More." She shimmied out of her shirt and threw it somewhere, missing the dresses Jaek had bought her. If she was in one of them, she would have been naked in one move.

Jaek's eyes flicked down her body and he licked his lips. Carise's complaints disappeared. She couldn't think of anything else but him.

He kissed her again while his fingers brought her nipples to stiff peaks. And though he was cautious at first, Carise's begging moans had Jaek learning she could take what his bruising fingers could give her. Never too much, not from him.

He'd never hurt her, and that reassurance made her brave.

And when he kissed his way down her body and let his lips take the place of his fingers, Carise saw stars. No man had ever worshiped her like this, taking his time to learn her body part by body part. He made a promise to every inch of her that she intended to make him keep.

And when she finally managed to get her pants off and lay naked beneath Jaek, she'd never felt more powerful.

Love made a person believe weird things.

Jaek's fingers teased her entrance, finding her dripping wet and ready for his cock. All of his cock, the substantial beast. He was proportionate, everything a seven-foot-tall alien should be. And Carise had the crazy idea that he might split her in two.

That concern must have shown on her face.

Jaek had a hand around his cock and it made it appear even bigger somehow. "We can stop," he said as he gave himself a stroke.

"Don't you dare." Carise dipped a hand down to her cunt and moaned at the sensation. "I want you, Jaek. All of you."

Any thoughts of stopping fled as Jaek brought her close, lifting her up until he fit himself at her entrance. She loved how he towered over her most of the time, but her only regret about it now was that they couldn't quite manage to kiss.

Then he eased himself inside of her and she was all pleasure.

Jaek took his time to stretch her, and her body adjusted, even if the press of him did have its uncomfortable seconds. But only seconds. And then she was fuller than she'd ever felt, closer to another person than she'd ever been, and she clung to Jaek as they moved together.

It started slow, but they were both starved after three weeks of separation and the desperation between them was too much. They moved quickly together, their bodies a slide of pleasure as they chased their release.

Carise didn't want it to end, even as she could feel her legs quake and the climax washing over her. She wanted to make this moment last forever, and she promised herself she would have more chances with Jaek.

She wasn't letting him go, not now that she'd found him again.

That was the thought she carried with her as she threaded her fingers with Jaek's and gave her body over to the pleasure, her body rippling around her alien's as she cried out his name and he emptied himself into her.

Sleep threatened to carry her away as Jaek pulled out of her and they settled in together, but Carise fought it. She was finally with Jaek again and she didn't want to waste a moment. She was worried that she might wake up and find out this was all a dream.

But she could feel the heat of Jaek's skin against hers and smell his masculine scent, and when she looked up and met his eyes, she could taste his kiss.

He was real. He was hers.

"I came for you that night," he said on a yawn. They were both fighting off the drowsiness of a good tumble, but it would pass. It had to. They had each other now.

Carise didn't want to talk about that day, she didn't want to remember it. But they had to. She'd wondered where Jaek had been. A part of her heart had broken when she hadn't seen him. But deep inside she'd been certain that something must have gone wrong. He wouldn't just walk away.

She licked her suddenly dry lips. "What happened? No one told me anything. I think Kenzie assumed I knew what was going on and she wouldn't let me get a word in edgewise. I only found out about the challenge and about Mad and Kenzie from Layala." It still burned to think of what her sister had kept from her.

Jaek tugged her close and recalled the story, from his discovery that she'd been taken to begging for Mad's help. And to the fight that had made him leave the palace that night. "I should have come back, or waited outside. But I was afraid my temper would get the best of me. I failed you."

She squeezed his arm and glared at him. "Failed? *Failed?* In a day you saw me rescued from an evil man and reunited with my sister, however briefly. Things may be a bit complicated at the moment, but I have hope now. Because of you."

"Why did you leave? That palace is one of the safest places on this cursed planet. And I've met your sister, she wouldn't let anyone lay a finger on you." His own fingers stroked up and down her back, and Carise was almost certain he was leaving some kind of mark. Not one that anyone would see, but one she would feel forever.

That was hard to think about and hard to explain. Her own mind had been such a jumble of emotions that night and morning that it sometimes felt like a nightmare. But she let herself be comforted by Jaek's touch as she tried to make sense of it all.

"Kenzie has a very... forceful personality. And I've

always been her little sister. Which was great when Henry Welser tried to steal my lunch money in elementary school, but it also meant half the kids at school were afraid to even *talk* to me for fear that they'd somehow upset Kenzie. Our dad... home wasn't great, and we had to fend for ourselves. *Kenzie* had to fend for us. And that night, when we were reunited, I could see it all starting again. She was planning to get us tickets back to Earth, to go back to our old lives like nothing had happened. And she didn't even bother to explain *how* she had saved me. And I feel like a little brat for running, but I wasn't ready to go. I couldn't leave y—" She cut off the last word.

Even laying in Jaek's bed, sweat cooling on her skin from their lovemaking, it felt somehow too revealing to finish that sentence.

"I wouldn't wish Guerran on anyone." Jaek kept stroking his hands on her back. "But I'm glad you're here."

There was more she could say, another confession she could make. The words hung between them. But it had been quite a long day, and she wanted nothing more than to curl up in Jaek's arms and sleep the night away.

Then she groaned, remembering.

"What?" Jaek snuggled against her, pulling the blanket up over them. "Is there trouble?"

"My roommate." Carise pushed at the blanket and pulled out of Jaek's embrace. He let her go and watched as she sat up. She looked around for her clothes and blushed to find them thrown across the room with abandon. "She might get worried if I don't show up. I don't want Layala to send people looking for me just because I didn't leave a note." She smiled down at her lover. "But I can come back tomorrow. And I'll leave a note this time. No worried roommate."

Jaek grabbed her hand and laced their fingers together, tugging her gently back towards the bed. "I'm sure your roommate can survive one night without you. Stay."

She wanted to. It would be so easy to give in to Jaek's smile and his warm body. If she stayed, they could kiss all night. And more. And already her body wanted more. She stood naked besides Jaek's bed and loved the way his eyes roved over her. There wasn't even a tiny part of her self-conscious about her nakedness and her scars.

But she had to be strong. "Layala has looked out for me. I don't want to worry her."

"Is Layala your roommate?" Jaek wasn't smiling anymore.

"No, but she works for her." Inspiration struck. "You could come back with me. Problem solved."

Jaek looked down at the bed and then back up at her. "Or we can stay in our warm bed and not give a damn about some roommate. It's late. Come on."

It wasn't, not really. It was only barely dark, and though Carise didn't relish walking through nighttime streets, she'd done it before. She was almost getting used to it.

"I have to go back," she insisted. She tugged her hand away from Jaek and scooped up her shirt, pulling it on. Her pants came next. Her shoes, bag, and shocker stick were by the door since she'd put all that stuff down when she arrived.

"Stay."

It sounded more like a command now, and the hair on the back of Carise's neck rose as her shoulders went up. "I didn't walk away from Kenzie just to take orders from someone else, Jaek. I'm going back to my apartment. I will see you tomorrow." Her hands shook a little as she laid that down, but her voice was steady.

"You're being ridiculous." Jaek pushed the covers back and got out of bed himself.

Carise really didn't have time to stare, and it undercut her argument. But he was a gorgeous man. And he was all hers.

She slipped on her shoes and grabbed her things. "Come see me tomorrow?" She didn't know what she would do if he said no. Stay? Maybe. Her willpower was hanging by a thread and her reasoning grew weaker by the second.

But she had to rely on herself. She couldn't just fall back into Jaek's bed as if she didn't have a life of her own.

Was that what this was about? Was her roommate just an excuse?

"I'll see you tomorrow," Jaek said. But he didn't sound happy about it.

She thought about giving him a final kiss, but kept

her distance. If she touched him again, she couldn't make herself leave.

Was it stupid to leave? Was she sabotaging herself?

She left. She had to go home.

But she'd only made it a short way down the path from Jaek's cave when two shadows crossed her path, and two hulking Kru'dari glared at her.

"We found her, boys."

17

JAEK KNEW he was being an idiot the second the door closed behind Carise. Yes, he wanted to spend the night with his mate gathered in his arms. He wanted to greet the morning with their bodies united together.

But he couldn't lock her up and throw away the key.

And he wasn't about to let her walk through the dark streets of Orion alone.

He scrambled to put on clothes and was out the door two minutes after her. She never had to know he'd followed her, so long as she made it home safe. Or perhaps he would take her up on her offer to go to her place. He'd like to see her bed.

But those thoughts fled when he heard her scream, and he ran.

Two men had cornered Carise and were trying to advance on her while she waved a large shocker stick in front of herself, keeping them away. The shocker stick was a deterrent, but it wouldn't hold them off for long. Especially since one good blow to her arm would send the stick flying.

A red wash of rage came over Jaek and he let his inner beast go. One of the men sensed him coming and ran.

The other wasn't so lucky. Jaek hit him with his full force and sent him tumbling to the ground.

The rock was an unlucky piece of terrain. The exile crashed into it, his head bashed open, and was gone before anyone realized it.

Jaek didn't mean to kill him, but he didn't regret it. He ignored the energy flowing out of the body. He didn't need it. Not with the way Carise's energy had flowed into him while they made love.

The fight ended before it started, but Jaek's adrenaline was still surging. He looked over his shoulder to see Carise standing behind him, her shocker stick gripped tight.

She hadn't run this time.

"Back to the cave," he said. It felt like there was gravel in his throat and it was difficult to say more.

This time Carise didn't argue. She looked down at the dead Kru'dari and then back up at him. She took a deliberate step towards him and grabbed his hand, raising it to her lips and kissing his knuckles.

"Thank you for saving my life." She turned back and went to the cave as instructed.

Jaek scowled in distaste at the exile on the ground. He'd have to take care of the body. There were no laws against murder on Guerran, no laws at all, really, but he didn't know if this exile had powerful friends who would want revenge.

And there was a bruise darkening the dead man's chin. He'd been the one to come for Carise earlier in the day.

A second attack wasn't a coincidence. And it certainly wasn't random.

Jaek ignored the sick sense of wrongness within him and quickly searched the man's pockets. He came back with a photograph that had a quick note scratched on the back. An address and a time frame.

The photograph was of Carise.

His rage threatened to take him again, but the man was already dead.

Jaek stuffed the picture in his pocket and dragged the man off the path and towards the trees. Someone was sure to find him. Or animals would get rid of him. If Carise wasn't waiting back home, Jaek would have made more of an effort, but she was more important.

He had blood on his hands again.

He wiped them on his dirty shirt and knew he'd have to consign the fabric to a fire. It was no great loss. He'd sacrifice much more to keep Carise safe.

When he entered the cave, she was curled up on his couch, staring at the wall as if it held the secrets of the universe. Jaek slipped off his shoes and then sat on the other side of the couch, leaving plenty of space between them.

He placed the photo on the table. "This was in his pocket. Did you recognize any of them?"

Carise shook her head, the movement so slight he would have missed it if he hadn't been staring at her intently.

"Has anyone else tried to attack you in the last weeks?" He'd been following—stalking—her as best as he could, and he hadn't seen anything. But he hadn't been there every minute.

"No." It was a whisper. She reached forward and snatched the picture off the table. "This was taken the day Jadirel took me. Must have been."

"How do you know?" He'd been so full of rage at the thought of someone tracking her down that he hadn't studied the photo for long.

"The dress. And the room. I don't remember someone taking a shot, but maybe it's from a security camera?" She flipped the picture over and read the back. "That's my address."

"You were a target. This wasn't random." He hated the way her shoulders slumped as he said what they both knew, but he needed her to understand. "You're in danger. More than you should be."

She flicked the photo back towards the table but overshot, and it floated to the floor. "I'm nobody! Just some human that had the misfortune to be plucked from home and passed around like an unwanted piece of trash." A sound caught between a laugh and a cry choked out of her. "Fuck! Why? Why, Jaek? I thought this was over."

Jaek was beside her in a flash, gathering her into his arms as she cried and holding her close. He wanted to promise that everything would be alright. He wanted to say that he could fix it.

But he didn't know how.

She'd been attacked twice in one day. There was no reason to think it would stop.

He could ask her questions, try to find the source. Perhaps her work for Layala had put her in the path of someone who'd want to collect her or harm her. Or perhaps the attack was aimed at her sister and Mad, and the mysterious attacker was getting to them through Carise.

Jaek didn't ask. She needed this cry, needed to let out these tears. And he doubted that anyone would dare attack them while they were safe in his cave. It was almost as well fortified as Mad's palace.

The stress of the day and the violence of the night eventually wore Carise out and she fell asleep in his arms. Jaek scooped her up and settled her carefully in his bed. He only hesitated for a moment before sliding in beside her.

He had missed her too much to resist the pleasure of sleeping beside her.

Some hours later he woke alone, but he could hear Carise walking around. When he got out of bed, he saw that her hair was damp and she'd appropriated his robe.

She was looking in his wardrobe and pulled out one of the dresses he'd bought for her, a small smile on her face.

He knew he should tell her that she could take them with, but he kept his mouth shut. He wanted her back in his home, in *their* home, and he wasn't about to start offering her to take things away.

"I should check in with Layala," Carise said as she chose a dress and closed the wardrobe. "And I should probably tell her about the attacks. She seems to know everything that goes on in Orion."

That she did, but that didn't mean that Jaek trusted her. He stepped close to Carise and wrapped his arms around her. "Is there any way I can convince you to stay here?" He didn't want her wandering around the city where anyone could do her harm.

But he wouldn't cage her.

Carise looked up at him and licked her lips, a small grin pulling at her mouth. "Don't tempt me."

She was temptation itself. And Jaek stole a kiss, but forced himself to make it quick. He pulled back and stepped away before he lost control, scooped her up, dumped her on the bed, and had his way with her. "We need to speak with Mad and Kenzie."

That hung between them for a moment, but Carise eventually nodded. "Those men could be attacking me to get to Kenzie or Mad."

"Yes." There was no way to sugarcoat it, so he didn't try. "Once you're done with Layala, I'd like you to head directly to Mad's palace. And if it's after dark, I want you to come with an escort. Once Layala knows you're in danger, she'll take steps to protect you. Will you let me keep you safe when you're not working?"

It tore something out of him to ask. She was his mate, even if she didn't know it. It was his right and his duty to keep her safe. Already her energy flew into him like the pathway between them had been created over years, and their bond wasn't even finished yet.

He needed to explain it to her soon, but dealing with the attacks was more important.

Carise pursed her lips and breathed deep, but she nodded again. "Very well. I won't do anything stupid. And *you* shouldn't provoke Mad. I expect you to be at the palace when I get there."

Jaek smiled and leaned close to kiss her again. He'd gladly accept this fierce protectiveness from his mate.

"I can escort you into the city," he said.

"Let me get changed, and then we'll go."

Jaek watched her, the entire time knowing the last thing he should do was let Carise out of his sight. But once she was ready, he led her into the city and knew he had to let her go.

She'd never stay with him if she didn't have her freedom.

18

Layala spotted Carise the moment she arrived at the café, and there was a strange look on her face. Was that surprise? Sure, Carise was running a bit late, but she didn't have strict hours. One of the perks of living on Guerran was that no one cared about a nine to five.

The place was busy, and Carise had to dodge her way to Layala's table where a familiar face was sitting beside her.

"My lovely messenger!" said Fynn, grinning up at her with a rakish smile. His eyes flicked up and down, taking in the dress she was wearing, and Carise wished she was wearing armor. Fynn's smile felt like a weapon.

"Hello," Carise greeted evenly. She had no idea who this guy was supposed to be, but he was trouble. He had to be. She looked at Layala. "Do you have a minute? I'd like to speak with you."

There was a commotion in the front of the cafe and

Layala scowled. "Keep him company while I deal with this." She got up from the table and forced her way through the crowded room.

"Ah, so nice to be alone." Fynn leaned close enough that she could smell whatever soap he used. It was nice. Not as nice as her Jaek smelled, though.

But he was too close. Carise took a chair and scooted it a foot away. Close enough to talk, but a bit too far to touch. "Is this your idea of alone?" There was a bit of a buffer around Layala's table, but they were still surrounded by people, mostly Kru'dari, but with more than a few humans and other aliens mixed in.

"Loneliness is a state of mind." He said it like it was meant to be profound.

Who was this guy supposed to be? Carise didn't like him, that was for sure. He was too slick, too flirtatious, and liable to bring trouble Layala's way. Not that she could warn him off. She was just a messenger. Layala was the spider at the center of the web.

The commotion at the front of the room died down, and Layala returned. "Help Ifan with the tables until I'm done with our guest here," she told Carise. "We'll speak later."

Carise wanted to object. She'd been attacked *twice* and was worried anyone could come up to her and start trouble. But Layala looked at her expectantly, and Carise turned and headed for the bar. She wouldn't be attacked in the heart of Layala's territory, someone would have to be crazy to do that.

But what were Layala and Fynn talking about? It wasn't like Carise had any business knowing, but she was curious. Ifan handed Carise a rag and told her to clean off tables, and Carise just *happened* to choose a table close to Layala and Fynn.

"That will be more than difficult," Layala was saying.

"Difficult is better than dead." Gone was the smiling, flirtatious Fynn. Now he was all business. "I won't last much longer."

"But you'll have to..." Layala angled herself differently, and Carise could no longer hear her.

Damn it.

Carise scrubbed down as many tables as she could and returned to Ifan for another assignment. Layala and Fynn talked for more than an hour, but Carise didn't hear any more.

At one point, Carise looked out the window and startled when she saw Jaek sitting at a table outside and sipping tea.

He was supposed to be talking to Mad, not stalking her. A part of her thought she should be angry, but instead some anxiety she hadn't realized she was feeling unknotted deep inside of her. He wanted to protect her, not control her.

God, that felt nice.

Fynn slipped away from Layala's table after a while, but he didn't leave, instead sauntering up to where Ifan was serving drinks at the bar and offering her a flirtatious smile.

Apparently Carise wasn't as special as she thought.

She glanced out again and grinned at Jaek, even though he wasn't looking at her. She was special enough.

Layala patted her on the shoulder from behind and Carise jumped in surprise, whipping around and nearly smacking her boss. Layala held up her hands, eyes wide. "Sorry," she said. "Didn't meant to startle you."

Carise's heart raced with the need to run, but she forced herself to calm down. "Right. It's okay."

"You wanted to talk?" Layala nodded back towards her table.

They sat, and Carise shivered at the memory of the night before. "I was attacked twice. Jaek found me and protected me. He killed one of the attackers. They had my picture." She laid it out as best she could, holding back her revulsion at the memories.

Layala nodded along as if this was no surprise. But Carise didn't know if the woman knew something or just had a very good poker face. "That's concerning. I don't like it when my people get hurt. I'll pull you off messenger duty for the next week or so and we'll see what we can find out."

Carise wanted to object. She liked roaming the city and learning it like it was her own. But she'd promised Jaek she wouldn't do anything stupid. So she wouldn't.

"Fugitive!" Two large Kru'dari exiles burst through the door and caught the attention of the entire room when one of them roared.

Carise shrunk down in her seat, unwilling to call any

attention to herself with the memory that the people who'd thought to hold her as a slave could still be looking for her.

But Fynn jumped up from where he'd slouched against the bar and took off running towards the back, knocking over a table and spilling a large pitcher of juice to the floor. He called something over his shoulder, but it was lost in the din of plates crashing to the floor.

The Kru'dari charged through, and Layala did nothing to stop them.

"That foolish man is going to get himself killed," she muttered just loud enough for Carise to hear.

She and Layala walked to the front of the cafe to see if anything else was disturbed, but all seemed fine. Layala nodded to where Jaek was standing, poised and ready for a fight that was apparently not coming.

"Why don't you go take your friend some lunch," she suggested. "It's been quite the morning. You could use a break."

Her stomach growled in agreement, and Carise turned, but before she could head to the bar to put in an order, Layala clamped a hand on her shoulder and squeezed hard. "Change of plans." Her voice had taken on an unexpected urgency. Layala was always calm. Carise had never heard her like this before. "Get to the palace. Run and don't stop."

She shoved Carise out the door to where Jaek was waiting and slammed the door. Carise heard the lock turn and looked at Jaek, wondering what had changed in two seconds.

Jaek tugged on her arm and nodded down the street to where five men were running their way, weapons bared and dangerous looks on their faces.

"That's her!" cried one of the men, pointing right at Carise. He had a scary looking club that had to be almost as big as she was. His friends all had clubs and knives, and they looked like they knew how to use them.

Jaek scooped her off her feet and ran.

19

JAEK's long legs ate up the distance to the palace far faster than Carise ever could, though he regretted that his hold on her couldn't be comfortable. Better a bit of discomfort than the loss of her life.

He dodged around corners and hoped the men in pursuit of them didn't have ranged weapons. Blasters weren't that popular on Guerran, but bows and crossbows were favored by some.

No bolts flew, so they'd been lucky.

He could feel the men gaining on them. They weren't hampered by Carise and they had to be able to guess where he was going, but he'd sacrifice anything he had to in order to get her to safety.

For a moment he considered putting her down and holding them off while she covered the rest of the distance to the palace, but he knew she wouldn't leave him and they didn't have time to argue.

It didn't matter. The palace was in sight and they just had to make it through the doors. Door that were guarded by two Kru'dari, one holding a wicked looking crossbow and the other with a sword that could do real damage up close.

And the guards were looking at Jaek and Carise like *they* were the ones who meant trouble.

"I'm Kenzie's sister!" Carise yelled at the top of her lungs without a word from Jaek. She could assess the situation as well as he could. "We're being chased!"

It caused just enough confusion for the guards to step aside and let them run through the doors. Jaek heard yelling behind them, but didn't turn back. The guard would handle their pursuers.

He hoped.

He didn't slow down until they burst into the throne room. Or rather, what used to be the throne room. Mad and Kenzie had redecorated. Jaek put Carise down as he took in the new room.

Guards jumped in front of him, and Jaek yanked Carise close to keep her from tripping into a wickedly sharp sword.

The throne that had once been central to the room had been cleared away, and now it looked more like one of the public grievance centers back on Krudare. Tables lined each wall with signs and stations for people to speak with Mad's representatives.

This was a place for the people of Mad's territory, not some room for him to exude his power.

But those people weren't in it now. Now it was mostly guards, along with Mad and Kenzie at the corner of the room. Kenzie held one of her knives and Mad had his axe. But Kenzie relaxed her grip when she realized Carise was with him.

"Stand down," Mad commanded, the words ringing out with the kind of confidence Jaek had never heard from him.

Kingship fit him well.

The guards glanced among themselves for a moment before lowering their weapons, but that only made the sounds from outside more obvious.

"We were chased here," Carise told her sister. "Your men engaged them at the door."

Kenzie took her word for it. "Go," she told the guards. "Clean up whatever mess there is."

The guards left the four of them alone. Jaek still had an arm around Carise, and he could feel Mad's and Kenzie's eyes on him like a brand. Forcing himself to step away was one of the hardest things he'd ever done, but Carise was safe now, and he wasn't going to start more trouble over half an embrace.

There'd be time to argue about *that* later.

Kenzie was staring at her sister with open longing and the kind of hurt on her face that only a loved one could inflict. But she blinked it away in an instant and Jaek wondered if he'd actually seen it at all.

He couldn't look at Carise's face. He didn't know

what he'd do if he saw that kind of heartbreak in her eyes.

"You said you were supposed to be safe." Kenzie's accusation was made calmly, but Jaek feared it wouldn't last for long.

"I was. For a bit." Carise let out a shuddering breath. She brushed her hand against Jaek's for just a moment before stepping across the room to get close to her sister. "I'm sorry I left like I did. I should have stayed and talked. I panicked. But we need help now, and I know you'll keep me safe. Right?"

"Always." The word choked out of Kenzie, and she pulled her sister close into an embrace strong enough to make Carise wince. She pulled back almost as swiftly and held up a hand. There was red on her fingers. "You're bleeding. You're hurt."

Carise brushed her own hand across her arm and found the blood. She looked back at Jaek. "Did they shoot at us? It doesn't hurt."

"That's the shock," said Kenzie before he could answer. She put an arm around her sister. "I'm getting you bandaged up." She looked at Jaek. "Report to Mad. We'll deal with the rest."

The sisters left.

And Jaek was left alone with Mad, the exile king who had banished him from this castle for daring to care about Carise.

His best friend.

His enemy?

Mad stared at him for a long moment before he let out a great sigh and his shoulders sagged. "Fuck," he breathed out. "My office." He tilted his head toward a discreet door.

Being in a small room with Mad was probably not the wisest idea. But he was completely under Mad's power anywhere in this castle. And so long as Carise was safe, nothing else mattered.

Mad pointed him at the padded bench that was pushed up against the wall and leaned against his substantial desk before reaching for a bottle of something dark red. He uncorked it and poured two glasses, handing one over to Jaek.

Krudare Red. The wine was treasured on Krudare and almost impossible to find on Guerran.

"Jadirel kept his cellars well stocked," Mad said as he sipped. "I'm using most of it for bribes to fix up this crumbling territory, but I've reserved a few bottles. Kenzie says it's good to be the king." He smiled when he said her name.

Jaek knew the feeling. Thinking of Carise made his heart light, and he wanted nothing more than to seek her out at this moment. She was bleeding and she needed tending to. But her sister would handle it. Speaking to Mad was his job now.

Mad's axe lay on the table behind him, the sharp blade a promise of violence. But Mad didn't look likely to reach for it. Nothing about his posture promised trouble. Of course, this was Guerran and that could change in an instant.

And he brimmed with power like Jaek had never seen it. He and Kenzie's mating bond was stronger than Jaek could have imagined. He hadn't met any other fated pairs on Guerran. There were those who entered into desperate bonds for what trickles of energy they could summon between them. But the bond between fated mates was something out of legend.

And he could still feel the whispers of Carise's energy within him. Energy he hadn't tried to summon from her. It had flowed freely. Just as energy from his mate might.

He really needed to talk to her about that.

"I overreacted that night," he forced himself to choke out. He wasn't sure he believed it, but Mad was an exile king now, and he'd need the apology. But if he commanded Jaek to kneel...

Jaek would do it. Because Carise needed him.

Mad sipped his wine. "So did I. And I'm sorry. You're the entire reason we found her. I didn't realize she was... she is your mate, yes?"

Jaek gulped down the wine before speaking. And when he finished the glass, he set it down carefully. But there was no other way to stall, and he wasn't sure why he should. "I think so."

"But the bond between you isn't sealed?"

"You're not the only ones she was avoiding. We only encountered each other two days ago." And he told the story as he knew it, only leaving out the private bits that Mad didn't need to know.

"You think someone is after Carise to get to me and Kenzie?" Mad asked.

Fury simmered in Jaek's veins. He hated to fight. He'd drawn more blood in the last day than he had in a year. But he'd do even more damage to keep Carise safe. "That's all I can think of. So how are we going to stop them?"

20

CARISE WINCED as Kenzie applied some kind of salve to her arm. Her dress was pulled down under her arm and she felt exposed to the cold air of the room, but it was only her and Kenzie in a surprisingly clean infirmary room. It looked like something that belonged on a much more civilized planet than Guerran.

"It just scratched you," said Kenzie, eyes intent on the wound. "Could have even been that you ran into something. Or they were shooting after you and it's a graze. But it's hard to miss an arrow. Maybe a slingshot."

She was talking more to herself than Carise, and Carise let her. Her sister seemed to have an encyclopedic knowledge of weapons and how they were used on Guerran. Carise would be happy to never think of weapons again.

How could she want to stay on this violent planet?

That was easy. Everyone she loved was here. And she'd seen worse.

Kenzie eased a sticky bandage onto her arm and helped Carise get her arm back into the sleeve. "There you go," she said. "Should be good as new in a day or two. That healing cream can work wonders."

"Thanks." Carise was sitting on a hard stool, and Kenzie stood between her and the door. Not that Carise needed to leave. Not yet.

They needed to talk.

Neither of them was eager to start.

Kenzie messed around with cleaning up the bandage wrappings and putting the healing cream back where it belonged. That only took a moment, but she took her time lining up a few containers that were on the table against one wall. She probably would have scrubbed the surface clean if she had a rag.

But all either of them had was each other and the heavy silence hanging between them.

Fine. This had to be done and it wasn't going to get any easier. "I meant it," Carise said, even as the words only felt half true. "I shouldn't have left like that. We should have talked."

"Yes, we should have." Kenzie leaned against the table, but the room was small enough that there wasn't much space between them. "I spent two years looking for you. Do you know what it felt like to have you disappear on me?"

Carise had to take a deep breath before she reflexively apologized. Kenzie could take on this tone that made Carise feel two inches tall. And she was using it now. And Carise *was* sorry. But that didn't mean she was completely wrong. "And I spent two years with all my choices being taken away, and then you showed up and started declaring exactly what was going to happen without bothering to ask me what I wanted." She couldn't look at Kenzie while she said it, instead staring at the gray floor.

But it had to be said. She'd written as much in her letter, but she wouldn't be a coward now and take those words back. She meant them.

Kenzie sucked in a loud breath, but she didn't say anything.

So Carise kept talking. "Jaek kept me safe for a while. It wasn't until you showed up that Jadirel took an interest in me."

"Fuck. Carise." Kenzie sounded like she'd been stabbed by those words, but Carise couldn't look up.

She pressed on. "I'm not saying that's your fault. *Thank you* for coming for me." She had to blink back tears as memories of her time in captivity tried to overwhelm her. But she wasn't going to let them. This talk was long overdue. "But when you found me, you didn't bother to explain what was going on. You just showed up and told me we were leaving. And now you've got this alien boyfriend—"

"Mate."

"What?" Now Carise did look up. "What's that

mean?" The word echoed in her mind and knocked her off track. Maybe the speech was too much.

Kenzie sighed. "Mad is my mate. Soulmates are real. At least for the Kru'dari. He's mine. I'm his. It's all very..." she scrunched up her nose in distaste, "romantic or some shit."

That startled a laugh out of Carise. But her mood quickly shifted. "How could you even *think* of giving that up? Why wouldn't you stay?"

"Because I thought you wanted to leave! How was I supposed to know you'd shacked up with some cave dwelling giant?" Kenzie's eyes were wide with anger and something Carise couldn't name.

"You could have asked." Her voice got small and she could feel herself shrinking. She'd gotten better at standing up for herself in the last three weeks. Really, in the weeks since she'd first been with Jaek. But Kenzie had been her big sister for twenty-four years and Carise couldn't break all those ingrained reactions.

Kenzie stepped back, and it was only then that Carise realized her sister had gotten closer. "Fuck, I'm sorry. You're right. I should have talked to you. I should have asked. And if you'd stayed around until morning, I would have."

"So this is all my fault now."

Kenzie didn't answer. Smart. She continued as if Carise hadn't spoken. "I didn't know what the situation was with Jaek. He decided to hide you away for his own reasons. I was going crazy with worry, and Mad had just challenged the king and won, and it was a lot in a few hours, and I acted poorly. You needed your rest. I made sure you got it. And we could have talked when we cooled down."

Carise listened. And what she heard sent a shiver down her spine. "You made sure I got my rest?" She didn't like the sound of that, and she hoped it didn't mean what she thought. "Kenzie, did you drug me?" Bile rose in her throat at the thought. She'd been drugged so many times by her captors that she'd grown to expect it.

But her sister?

And Carise *had* gotten really sleepy after her talk with Kenzie.

Kenzie froze where she stood, as if that would somehow make her invisible to Carise. She swallowed and her throat bobbed. "I had the servant put melatonin in your wine. To help you sleep. That's it. It wasn't a sedative."

"So that makes it better?" Carise shot up from her chair and scowled at Kenzie, even as tears threatened to fall. "You *drugged* me in the same palace where some insane man chained me up. And you're trying to make *me* feel bad that I ran? How dare you? If I wanted something, I would have asked for it." She didn't let herself wonder if she would have been able to sleep that night without help, that wasn't the point.

This was just one other way Kenzie had stepped into her life and tried to take over, as if Carise wasn't a full-grown adult. As if she couldn't make her own choices.

"I'm here because we need your help," Carise spat at her sister. "I think someone's trying to use me to hurt you. And right now, I'm tempted to walk out that door and let them. But no one will ever own me again. So clean up your mess. I can't even look at you."

Carise walked out of the room as tears fell down her cheeks. She didn't know where she was going, but the palace was big. And she wanted to hide forever.

21

CARISE FOUND a little alcove with an uncomfortable bench and curled up on it, clutching her legs to her chest and resting her face on her knees. The tears had gone just as quickly as they'd come on, but her whole body felt carved out, like someone had taken a knife and sliced out all the good bits.

How could Kenzie do that?

She'd been betrayed by her own sister and wanted to run. If someone gave her a ticket to a spaceship off this planet right then, she probably would have taken it.

So that's what you do now? Some mean voice in the back of her mind demanded. *Things get tough and you run away? Is that all you are?*

The problem with the voice in Carise's head was that she couldn't talk it down. Or run away from it. It followed her wherever she went. And it sounded a lot like the stronger woman she wanted to be.

Maybe Guerran wasn't the place for her. Maybe she couldn't live in the same city as Kenzie while all this anger roiled within her. Or maybe Carise needed to give it some time and not make any rash moves.

Again.

Footsteps echoed down the hall coming her way and she tried to shrink into the shadows. Guards and servants walked the hallway every so often, and a few had glanced at her, but none had bothered her. That was a small favor.

But she recognized those footsteps. Jaek slipped into the alcove and leaned against the wall. There wasn't enough room for him on the bench, the way she was sitting. Carise probably should have shifted herself so he could sit, but she stayed where she was.

"Talk went bad?" he asked quietly.

Carise nodded against her knees.

"Want to go hide in my room?" There was no judgement in the offer.

And some of that hollowness felt like it was filling up with Jaek's kindness. Carise reached a hand up, and Jaek linked their fingers together and tugged her up. She might have even let him carry her if he tried, but the man was wise enough not to.

Probably for the best.

He didn't say anything as he led her down winding halls and came to a solid wood door that opened under his touch. "Mad said he'd have quarters made up for each of us," he said as he led her inside and closed the door behind her.

"I don't know where mine are." Kenzie probably would have told her. Or she would have had a servant take her there. How crazy was that? Her sister had freaking servants.

Jaek was holding himself rigid a few feet away from her. Energy seemed to vibrate under his skin, and she wondered if he wanted to go and fight her battles or if it was something else.

She didn't ask.

"Do you want to find your room?" he asked quietly.

"I want to be with you." He was her constant on this planet, the one person she trusted wholeheartedly. He'd never tried to cage her, he certainly hadn't tried to *drug* her, and his presence grounded her in ways she didn't understand.

Jaek was beside her in two steps, gathering her into his arms and hugging her tight. Carise clung to him. She didn't cry. Her tears were gone, and in their place was simmering anger that was sure to boil over again at some time, but she didn't want to be angry anymore either.

She just wanted Jaek.

She hadn't paid much attention to the room they were in, but what could she miss? It was a bedroom. There was a bed. That was all that mattered. She went on her tiptoes and guided Jaek's head down, capturing his mouth in a fierce kiss.

He was still for a moment, that control of his will as strong as iron. But everything had a breaking point, and she felt it the second Jaek's snapped. Felt it and triumphed.

He scooped her up, and she wrapped her legs around his waist as best she could, even though he was so big that it was a challenge in and of itself. He was a tower of strength, and he was giving it all to her as his kiss imprinted itself on her soul.

She'd give him anything he asked for. She'd gladly go back to his home now and never leave. But Jaek didn't say anything; he just kept kissing her as if his life depended on it.

She felt *alive*, blood rushing through her veins and practically fizzing with excitement. It was always like that with Jaek, but today it was even more. Was it that her emotions were already running high? Was it something in the air on Guerran?

Soulmates are real.

She didn't want to dwell on any of her conversation with Kenzie, but that thought barreled into her and didn't let her go. Not as Jaek kissed her like he belonged to her, not as he laid her down on the bed.

Not as he tore off her shirt and loomed over her like a barbarian raider.

Could he be hers?

If she was brave, she might ask. She might dare to hope. But the threat of disappointment was too much, and Carise couldn't take anymore today. Not after the attacks.

Not after Kenzie.

Then Jaek shucked off his pants, and all thought of her sister and any of her problems fled.

He was a beautiful man. Technically *not* a man, since he wasn't human, but that wasn't the important part. He was all male, and all there for her pleasure. The height was daunting, even if she felt protected when he towered over her. The muscles were a promise of the strength he'd use to defend her from her enemies.

And his cock was a promise of something else entirely. He had his hand wrapped around it and gave his thick length a stroke, looking down at her, eyes dark with pleasure.

Carise still wore her dress, though it wouldn't take much to just hitch it up and let him have his way with her.

But they were in a well-fortified bedroom. There'd be no more attacks tonight. And she wanted to bare herself to him as completely as she could.

This wasn't their first time. But last night, something desperate had overtaken her, and she'd surrendered to the madness of passion. Now she wanted to savor the time she had with Jaek.

She sat up and jerked off her dress, tossing it somewhere it would be out of the way. She didn't have on any underwear, something that might have been a nuisance at another time, but now felt like miraculous foresight. In one move she was naked under Jaek's gaze, and she could bask in it.

She wasn't a person who reveled in nakedness. She didn't like to feel exposed. But Jaek's tender gaze was the farthest from exposure it could be.

The man made her feel precious.

He made a noise deep in his throat as he took in her nakedness, and if she laid back, he'd take her right there. She wasn't complaining, but she wanted to take her time to explore.

He'd already had his chance.

She scooted forward on her knees and tried not to think of how ridiculous the move looked before she wrapped her fingers around Jaek's cock and tugged him forward until she had him laying down on the bed and under the gentle power of her fingers.

It had to be torture, the way she gently brushed her fingertips over his length, exploring the texture, the veins and ridges of his cock, and taking her time. She could feel him straining against some great force, but he laid there and let her do her worst.

He'd never rushed her before. Why would he start now?

When she brushed her thumb over the head of his cock, his hips jerked and the sound he growled out was a tortured moan of pleasure. Carise flicked her eyes up and saw him watching her intently.

"You undo me." Jaek made the confession like it was his darkest secret and a gift only for her.

And his words were their own kind of challenge. She grinned at him and knew it was playful, something she hadn't felt in a long time. She leaned down and licked her tongue across the head of his cock, grinning even more when Jaek cursed.

She wanted him completely undone.

She couldn't say she had much skill when it came to this, but she wanted to give this to Jaek, and for herself she wanted to explore him even further, to see and feel and taste the things she could do to and for him. This was a sharing of their bodies, and there was no part of him that she wanted to miss out on.

But Jaek was big, and she only had so much mouth.

She took the head of his cock in her mouth and played with it, her tongue laving at the hot surface. Jaek's hips hitched just enough to let her know she was doing something right, but he practically plastered his hips to the bed to keep from doing any more.

Good.

They could do *that* another time.

She wrapped a hand around his base and took her time, loving the gruff curses he spat out and the way she felt like she had total control of him. There was power in this act and she felt like a goddess.

But she had to pull back before long. The night wasn't over. Not by a long shot.

She made her way up Jaek's body, trailing kisses and

running her fingers through the hair on his chest. It was thick and dark and she loved it. She loved everything about Jaek.

Before she could follow that line of thought completely, Jaek captured her with a searing kiss. They were already so close, but not close enough. She wanted him deep inside of her and claiming her as his.

She wanted everyone to know that they belonged to one another, whatever that meant, whatever they had to do.

But most of all, she just wanted him.

They couldn't stop kissing, even as they had to strain because of the height difference. The bed made it better, but it was impossible to forget he was her giant.

And then he rolled her over and Carise forgot about everything else as Jaek teased her slick entrance, the blunt head of his cock a hard promise of pleasure.

He took her slowly, so slowly she almost begged him for more. But there was something in Jaek's eyes, a need she couldn't put into words, that kept the words down. And from the slow way pleasure rolled through her body, she could savor the moment.

She'd savor every moment with him.

The pleasure built so subtly she almost didn't realize, but when it crashed through her, she was wrecked, calling out his name and clutching at him, forgetting everything except this moment with her alien lover.

Troubles waited on the other side of the door. She'd

have to face her sister, and the threats that lurked on the streets of Orion.

But not yet. Now she let Jaek gather her close and hoped she could pretend the rest of the world didn't exist.

Just for a little while.

22

Jaek didn't want to leave Carise, even for a minute, but the day had been long and they both needed food. He shifted himself out of the bed as she slept and looked down at her for several long moments.

She was peaceful in sleep, the troubles wiped away as she dreamed. He wished he could give her that peace while she woke, but she wouldn't be safe until this latest catastrophe was dealt with.

And as he walked down the hall, his own brain whirred with a different catastrophe. He could feel her energy in his veins, even stronger than before. He didn't think the mate bond was completed between them. As far as he knew, she had to accept it from him, and how could she accept something she didn't even know existed?

But every moment he didn't tell her about it felt more

like a betrayal. She deserved the full truth from him. He couldn't be another person to disappoint her.

If her sister had been in that hallway when he found Carise, he might have done damage and faced the consequences from Mad later. Those tears could kill a man.

Instead he had given his mate the only thing he had: himself.

A part of him was tempted to turn on his heel, march back into the room, and declare all so that the air between them would be clear of any dishonesty. Carise had been adamant that she was entitled to know everything, and she was right.

But Jaek kept moving towards the kitchen. For one, his Carise was sleeping and while he knew he should tell her all, it didn't mean he needed to disturb her sleep. And second, his stomach was in knots of hunger, and confessing that Carise owned his soul was not something to be done on an empty stomach.

And there was something else. Everything in his mate's life was precariously balanced or in the process of falling down. She'd started to work for Layala, though Jaek had to doubt Layala's motives. She'd found housing of her own, even if he wanted his mate in his own quarters at his side. And she'd spoken with her sister, though that might have done more harm than good.

But Carise was trying to take control. How would she feel if he told her fate had come between them and meant to bind them together?

He wanted her. Forever. There was no doubt in his

mind. And he would have wanted her without The Want, the urge that came upon Kru'dari when they met their fated mates.

Bur Carise's choices had been ripped away from her so many times. Would she feel forced if he told her? Would she be tempted to run since it was the one way she'd found to assert any kind of control?

By the time he made it to the kitchens, mostly by instinct and smell since he didn't actually know the layout of Jadirel's—now Mad's—palace, Jaek's stomach was knotted for entirely different reasons, and he wasn't sure if he could eat.

When he stepped through the door, no one was there. Night had fallen and most of the palace was likely asleep. Good. He wasn't in the mood for others.

He found a large bowl that would work to hold a decent amount of food and started picking through the cold box, finding cheeses he knew Carise liked and some of the more delicate fruits that withered in days if not chilled. He felt a bit like a thief in the night, but didn't let that stop him when he heard the hallway door open and shut.

He turned and there was Kenzie.

She wore thin pants and a sleeveless top, and only had one knife on her hip. Pajamas, then. She watched him gather his feast and didn't say anything.

Jaek could walk away. He and Kenzie did not have a positive history of interaction. And Kenzie had to know that Carise was sleeping in his room. There were no secrets from the queen of this palace. But Kenzie's hand didn't go for her knife, and when their eyes met, she looked so pained that Jaek felt her sorrow stab him in the gut.

He put the bowl down and leaned against the counter behind him. He crossed his arms but didn't speak.

Kenzie slid onto a stool and rested her elbows on the preparation table. Then she looked up at him. "Is she okay?" He'd heard men sentenced to death who sounded better than her. Misery laced every word, and he had no doubt she'd been torturing herself since her conversation with Carise.

Jaek owed her nothing. He could refuse to talk now and go back to his mate and let Kenzie stew. A part of him thought she deserved it for whatever she'd done. Carise hadn't taken the time to explain, and he didn't need the details.

But he also knew that Kenzie had crossed the galaxy to find Carise and that she'd do anything for her. Whatever mistake she'd made, it was out of love, not malice. And he didn't want his mate estranged from the only family she had.

So Jaek answered. "She's asleep. I think she'll be hungry when she wakes up." He tilted his head towards the bowl of food.

"She likes cheese," Kenzie muttered, and it might have been a peace offering.

"I know."

She jerked a bit at the reminder that Carise was no stranger to Jaek, but nodded after a moment. "I never wanted to hurt her."

"I know that, too." No one capable of supreme malice could look so miserable. "But she's angry right now and she needs time. Whatever you did—"

"She didn't tell you?" Kenzie was shocked.

How could he phrase it delicately? "We didn't say much before she fell asleep." Technically true, if leaving out something important. But he had no interest in sharing intimate secrets with Kenzie.

But from the way her eyes widened a fraction, she understood. "I see."

"She told me a bit. Before we got here. I'm guessing there's more?" It wasn't much of a guess, seeing as Carise had seemed ready to forgive Kenzie before they arrived and now, he didn't know if she could face her sister.

Kenzie just nodded.

"She's a good woman. And she loves you. Give her time. And space. She's changed since you knew her, but that doesn't mean she's not still your little sister." He didn't love talking, especially not with people who hurt his mate, but this needed to be said. Carise needed this.

"Do you think I don't know that?" Kenzie snapped, one hand sliding off the table, probably going for her knife. Then she got control of herself and placed both hands back on the table to show she was unarmed.

"I think you've both changed. And you need to figure out who you are now. There's no going back." He picked up the bowl of food and left the kitchen before Kenzie could try and talk more. Or stab him.

He'd said what needed to be said. That was all there was to it. And he wasn't about to waste time talking to Kenzie when he could be with Carise.

That was where he belonged.

23

CARISE WOKE up when she heard the door shut. And there was Jaek, standing right in front of it and holding a bowl. "What have you got there?" she asked, blinking away sleep. She had no idea what time it was, but she felt more rested than she expected to after everything that happened with Kenzie.

Sex was great for relaxation.

Jaek held up the bowl before setting it down on her bedside table and leaning over to kiss her. Carise tried to pull him down on top of her, but the man resisted when her stomach growled.

Stupid stomach.

He pulled back with a smile. "I brought food."

She looked at the bowl and furrowed her brow. There were three blocks of cheese and a handful of fruits she couldn't identify. One looked like a clump of lemons that had all grown together and been cursed by an evil demon. The other fruit looked like if peaches and strawberries somehow had a baby and that baby was blue and glowed with an inner light.

She picked up one of the strawberry/peach things and ran her thumb over it. "Is this a fruit I have to peel, or can I just take a bite?" When unsure, it was best to ask. And she hadn't survived this long on alien food by being incautious.

Jaek picked up a twin to her fruit and bit into it, letting a bit of juice run down his face. "Just bite." He circled around the bed and lay beside her while he ate his snack.

It felt almost wrong to be snacking on pilfered fruits and cheeses while lying naked in bed in the *palace* her sister was somehow in charge of, but it wasn't quite the strangest thing that had happened in Carise's life, so she decided to go with it.

She bit into the fruit and was pleased at how sweet it was, even if it was a bit too juicy to eat cleanly in bed. She had to lick off her fingers to keep from becoming a sticky mess. And when she caught Jaek watching her, she might have slowed down just to ensure she did a thorough job.

He breathed in sharply, but didn't reach for her.

There'd be time for that later.

She nibbled on more food and felt better with every bite. Halfway through her makeshift meal, she was surprised to realize that she didn't ever suspect Jaek of drugging it. Of course, she'd learned to trust him and he had no reason to.

But Kenzie should have been trustworthy too.

She put the cheese she was eating aside, no longer hungry.

Jaek watched her for several moments before he spoke. "Your sister was in the kitchen," he admitted, like it was a great crime. "We spoke. Briefly."

"And did she tell you I was being a petulant child and throwing a tantrum?" It came out harsher than Carise intended.

"She looked miserable."

Why did that hurt more? "I'm supposed to be mad at her," and yet her heart ached. "She *drugged* me. She took away my choice. And one word that she's hurting and I want to run out there and tell her it's all right." Carise tried to scrunch up into a ball, but the blanket got in the way. "God, I'm weak."

"You're not weak." Jaek pulled her close, holding her tight, and she fit in his arms like she was made to be there. "She drugged you?" There was a thread of unrelenting fury in the question.

And Carise had to be fair. She always was when it came to her big sister. "Sort of? She slipped melatonin into my wine after she rescued me. It helps people sleep, but it's not really a sedative. It's probably no stronger than if I'd had a second glass of wine that night."

Now she was making excuses for Kenzie. Carise really was pathetic.

"But having a second glass of wine would have been your choice. Same as asking for that drug. It doesn't matter that it was weak. She didn't ask." Jaek squeezed her *almost* too tight, but stopped before his grip was too much.

And he got to the heart of her problem. "Am I weak if I forgive her?" Carise needed the answer, and she wanted someone to give it to her. Making decisions was *hard*, and she was still out of practice.

"You're not," Jaek assured her. "You're so strong, you just can't see it yet."

"And am I a terrible person if I can't forgive her?" That was the bigger fear. What Kenzie had done stabbed Carise to her heart, even if she could see *exactly* why her sister had done it. But Carise's choices had been taken away so many times, and she couldn't get back at most of the people who'd done that to her.

She could get back at Kenzie.

"No, you're not." Jaek kissed the top of her head. "But you don't have to make a decision today. Or even anytime soon. Kenzie knows she screwed up. She'll give you the space you need. And if you can't forgive her... Well, that's her problem. She's the one who did wrong."

Tears threatened, but not the wracking sobs of earlier. She pushed them down. She'd cried enough for half a lifetime. "How did you end up on Guerran? You're the nicest criminal I've ever met." As soon as she said it, she realized how bad that sounded. "Oh my God, I'm so sorry. You know—"

Jaek leaned down and kissed her before she could say anything else, and when he pulled back, he was smiling, even if there was a tinge of sadness in his eyes. "It's okay. I understand what you mean."

That was a relief. And Carise kept her mouth shut before she could say anything stupid.

"It was seven years ago," he started. His voice took on a distant tone, like he was diving back into the memory. Carise leaned in close to make sure he could feel her and keep him grounded. "I don't have family back on Krudare. Never did. At least, not since I was so young that I can't remember. And I got big young. There were other kids who stayed small, and they needed protection. We all banded together and did what we could for one another. But life is tough on Krudare for a bunch of coin-less orphans. We did small jobs, whatever we could, for food or shelter or the occasional coin, but there was never enough. So stealing food from local markets was what we had to do. I'd been doing it for years at that point. It wasn't difficult. Someone stands lookout, someone causes a distraction, I nab the food, we all run and feast. One night it went wrong. The others got away because I stayed back to hold off the guard. We fought. And it was so *easy* to hit him. It was like the part of me that knew it was wrong disappeared. It's why I hate fighting. I always come back to myself, and there's bloodshed and death and it's all my fault."

He shook his head and continued. "The guard wasn't alone. His backup came and took me into custody. The guard survived, so I escaped execution. They cut me off from the Fount and sent me to Guerran with a half-empty Pitcher. A year later I met Mad, and we've been friends since. It's... not as bad as I feared. And in some ways worse."

"What's the Fount? What's a Pitcher?" The rest of his story made her heart hurt, but Carise had never heard of the Fount. It sounded important.

Jaek looked at her for a long second, confused. Then he blinked it away. "Right. You're human. Of course you wouldn't know. Krudare has energy running through it that all Kru'dari can access. There's no way to stop it. It sustains us, makes us stronger, faster, more alert. But when we leave the planet, we're cut off from it. There are ways to store a bit of that energy for short periods, but never for long—those are called Pitchers. There are only a few available on all of Guerran, and exiles do more than kill for them. Most planets don't have anything like the Fount. Guerran certainly doesn't. That's the real punishment of exile. The only ways of eking out energy here are fighting or fucking. And even the fucking is kind of violent."

"So when we..." Carise looked down at the bed, her cheeks heating. "That gave you this energy? You sucked it out of me like an energy vampire?" That felt like something out of a TV show. "But I feel fine." And there was nothing violent about it.

He shifted, angling his body closer to her. "There's something I need to—"

Lights and sirens blared.

Carise clamped her hands over her ears. "What's that?"

"We're under attack."

24

Jaek wanted Carise to stay in the room, but they both jumped out of the bed and threw on whatever clothes they could find. He didn't stop her from leaving with him. They needed to find out what was going on. Right now, the sirens blaring were a warning; they'd be much more insistent if the walls had been breached.

He hoped.

Besides, there was likely to be a well-defended place for non-combatants, and *that* was where he wanted his mate holed up, not in some barely defended room where anyone could find her.

The central room was full of guards rapidly arming and getting into battle gear, but Jaek didn't immediately see Mad. Then he noticed the door to Mad's office was cracked open and led Carise through the throng.

Mad was holed up with Kenzie and more men that Jaek recognized from Jadirel's rule. These exiles hadn't been high up in the ranks; they'd been too unwilling to do Jadirel's dirty work.

And now they were working for Mad. Interesting.

Kenzie's shoulders sagged in relief when she saw Carise come in behind him, but she didn't make another move to greet her sister. Carise gave Kenzie a nod, but Jaek was sure part of her wanted to spring across the room and hug her sister tight.

"What's going on?" he asked, the words coming out more of a demand than was wise when speaking to an exile king.

But Mad didn't stand on ceremony. He had his huge axe slung across his back and wore his battle leathers. He'd be a gruesome sight on the battlefield. "We're trying to find out. We've got angry exiles outside, but they've only triggered the perimeter defenses. They aren't inside."

"You're sure?" Not his place to question it, but he had Carise to keep safe.

"Certain," Mad confirmed.

"Could this be someone trying to challenge you?" Kenzie asked, face worried and hand stroking the hilt of her knife.

"Not likely." This came from one of the exiles, Daryux. "They'd need to get face to face to issue a challenge. This is a siege."

That hung in the air for a moment before Mad gave a decisive nod. "We're built to withstand that. Unless they've got a secret weapon, but there's no reason to think they do. Most of the men are in the palace, and we're safe enough for now. But I don't want anyone leaving without an order to do so. We're going to have to see how this plays out."

He turned to Daryux and his companion. "I want you two to rally the guards and set up a defense. Give me options if things take a turn. And don't provoke anyone outside. Right now they're angry, but they're not fighting. Yet. Let's see if we can stop this."

There was a roar from outside. "Attack!" came the call from the clustered guards.

"So much for that," Mad muttered. "Get us a defense, Daryux, buy us time. I want this resolved with as little bloodshed as possible."

Daryux and his companion looked uncertain, but they both nodded and left.

"How can I help?" Carise asked before Jaek could figure out where they were letting the non-combatants shelter. "I know I'm not a fighter, but surely you need people who don't carry knives."

He couldn't tell if that was meant to be a jab at Kenzie or not, and Kenzie didn't seem to take it that way. "Kitchens," Kenzie said. "We'll need food, and there will be a makeshift infirmary if this goes on longer than a few minutes. Welcome to our first battle." Kenzie turned to Mad and gave him a searing kiss. "You know where I'll be." And she was off.

Jaek looked at Mad, and an unspoken conversation

passed between the two of them before he turned to Carise. "I'll show you to the kitchens."

They walked slower now. Very distantly there was a faint clash of weapons, but deep in the palace they were safe for now. Stars above, Jaek wanted to wrap Carise up and keep her safe and protected from the violence to come.

She'd never forgive him.

They made it to the door and he could hear activity behind it. "Here we are," he said. "I'm sure you'll be able to help."

Carise looked at the door and then back at him. Then she went on her tiptoes, dragged his head down, and gave him a searing kiss. "I just found you. You better not die." She kissed him again. "I love you."

But before Jaek could say anything, the door burst open and someone who might have been a cook on a normal day smiled brightly when she spotted Carise. "Good, we need help, get in here." She clamped her hand on Carise's arm and dragged her into the kitchen.

It was the final good part of Jaek's day, and he held it close to his heart, knowing he'd need it for the darkness ahead.

By the time he made it back to Mad, the mood had changed and the guards had thinned out. "Let's do this," Mad told him with a grim smile. "I can't keep the nice house if I can't defend it."

"I didn't think we'd ever end up here." Jadirel had been a cruel exile king, but neither Jaek nor Mad had seriously considered challenging him. Not until he forced their hand.

Or, well, Mad's hand. Jaek had little to do with it.

They followed the flow of soldiers to the sounds of the fighting, and once they were outside, Jaek's heart sank. This wasn't some small contingent of agitated exiles.

This was an army.

A small one, but still. They'd been pushed back beyond the alleys and streets that ringed the palace, and archers and exiles with crossbows were set up and taking out whoever they could that came into range.

There was no more time for talking. The crossbows couldn't take out everyone, and there were enough soldiers brave enough to charge the line. Fighting was fierce, and the opposing soldiers were smart enough to engage and then retreat, rather than let themselves be struck down.

The call of battle sang to Jaek, that temptation of violence that he tried so hard to suppress. But if there was ever a time for it, it was now. The enemy was fast approaching, and all that stood between his mate and their fury was Jaek's fists and the palace walls.

Mad seemed to procure a new axe from nowhere. "I thought you might want this. Vent your frustration."

Very much. Jaek took it, and let the battle take him.

Time lost its meaning as he took out his fury on the exiles who dared attack Mad's palace. He barely felt the nicks and scrapes that came from engaging, and blood pooled at his feet as his enemies fell.

Eventually someone took his place on the line, and he was pulled back, bandaged, given water, and time to rest. The sun was beginning to rise and the battle still raged on.

How long had it taken?

How long could it last?

When given the signal, Jaek switched places again and dove back into the fray. On the other side of the battle, Jaek could see a cluster of Kru'dari, and he thought he recognized Baryn, a favorite of the dead exile king Jadirel.

Was this his battle? Or had he found a new leader to follow?

Jaek pulled back from the fighting to find Mad. Baryn shouldn't have been much of a threat. Not at most times. But the army on the streets in front of the palace was proof enough that the issue was real.

Plenty of soldiers and guards were injured, but Jaek didn't see many bodies. A few forms were crumpled on the ground, unlucky blood sacrifices to the battle, and there would be more to come. This fighting had the feel of a distraction, and Jaek couldn't help but wonder what came next.

He didn't want to find out.

Mad had pulled back. Blood welled on his forehead from an untended cut and he looked fierce. Beside him, Kenzie was cursing at a medic as a cut on her arm was sealed and bandaged. It had to be taking all of Mad's considerable strength not to banish his mate back into the building, but he didn't.

Jaek couldn't do that. If he saw Carise out here, his only concern would be for keeping her safe. And lucky for him, his mate was no warrior. He could fight battles for both of them.

"Report," Mad snapped when he saw Jaek.

"I think I saw Baryn across the street. He's not engaging, but he seems happy to send fighters towards us." He gladly accepted a bottle of water and downed it between words. Fighting was thirsty work.

"Baryn? That's the guy I beat in the pit, right?" Kenzie hissed and cursed as the medic finished with her bandage as she spoke.

"The same," Mad confirmed.

Jaek had heard of the fight. Most of Guerran had. But he hadn't seen it. It must have been a sight. "Could be he's not brave enough to mount a one-on-one challenge," Jaek offered. If Kenzie could take Baryn in a fight, Mad certainly could as well.

Before Mad could say anything, there was a loud whizzing sound. "Take cover!" someone yelled.

They dived for cover as a projectile flew overhead and smacked into the castle walls. Jaek braced for an explosion, but none came. And after a few moments, he deemed it safe enough to look. The walls had been dented, but the structure stood.

For now.

"Looks like they're tired of one-on-one fighting." Mad grimaced. "Daryux!" He called for his trusted guard who joined them a moment later. "Let's show them what we've got."

Daryux grinned, and Jaek had never been happier to be on the same side as Mad. He didn't want to face whatever Daryux was about to throw at their enemy.

25

Carise almost fell over into a ball of fear when something slammed into the palace walls. She wasn't the only one. There might not have been any battle inside, but the hallways were a swarm of activity of people bringing things to the battle and shuttling the worst of the wounded to the makeshift infirmary.

She was too busy to worry. And she had full faith in Jaek. And Kenzie. And, by extension, Mad. They wouldn't let one little battle oust them from power.

As she ran a basket full of fully stocked medkits to the battle, she saw a few men run down the hall. They looked like Kru'dari and weren't wearing the uniforms of servants, which was strange. Most of the Kru'dari were letting blood in front of the palace.

But she didn't know everyone, and she didn't have time to question it. Once she'd dropped off the kits, she took a moment to catch her breath. And then she could have sworn she saw smooth talking Fynn.

What? Since when did he work for Mad?

She followed after him for a few paces without a thought and then paused. The hard-faced cook would have *words* if Carise took her sweet time getting back. But something struck her as odd, and she had to follow her gut.

What if the bad guys had gotten into the palace?

Probably she should raise the alarm, but she didn't think they could afford to lose any guards from the battle, and she didn't want to cause a stir if it was just her mind playing tricks on her. She wouldn't get close enough to be in any danger, she promised herself. She just wanted to take a look.

So she snuck down the nearest hallway, and there was Fynn. He ran a hand through his hair and looked more ragged and desperate than she'd ever seen him. And he spotted her the second she rounded the corner.

So much for not getting caught.

"There you are!" He grinned, but it just looked tired. "Come quick, I need your help."

"You work for Mad?" Maybe if she'd actually been in the palace in the last three weeks, she would have known that, but there was no fixing it now.

"I'm here, aren't I?" Fynn waved her forward. "Come on. I've got an injured woman that needs tending. Human. Brown skin. Tons of knives on her. Please, hurry. She's hurt."

Kenzie.

Fynn could be lying to her. Even as her heart rate kicked up and worry for her sister flooded her veins, Carise realized it. But if he was telling the truth, she'd never forgive herself if she turned back and let her sister suffer.

What if Kenzie was dying?

Carise couldn't let that happen. Not with how she'd left things between them.

"What happened?" she asked as she followed Fynn down the halls. She hadn't heard anyone bring Kenzie in, but they could be keeping it quiet, especially if they didn't want morale to suffer.

"There's a battle going on out there. People get hurt." He sped up and Carise got disoriented. She didn't see anyone else, and that was weird.

This was wrong.

She stopped moving, but Fynn only went a few more steps before he came to a thick, metal door. "She's out here," he said.

"No she's not." Carise backed up a step as shame washed through her. How could she have let herself fall for this? Fynn *had* to be lying to her. If Kenzie was actually hurt, she'd be in the infirmary receiving the best medical care that Mad could offer.

The friendly look slid off of Fynn's face and he was on her before she could run away, clamping a hand on her arm and dragging her to the door. "It's not personal," he said, dropping any pretense that this wasn't a trap. "It's just Guerran."

He opened the door, which led out into a small courtyard. She didn't see another way out of the courtyard, but Fynn dragged her across and pushed away a bit of greenery to reveal a break in the wall that was barely big enough for a person to scramble through.

She wondered why the people attacking the palace weren't trying to sneak through that hole, but she didn't give Fynn the satisfaction of asking. She wasn't going to cry or beg.

She had to find a way out of this.

Her vision was going gray around the edges and it was hard to breathe. She remembered what it was to be chained up and at another person's command, and she didn't want to go through that again. She wouldn't survive.

Her life had finally been starting to make sense. She thought she could be happy.

Once she was firmly through the wall and on the ground, she kicked Fynn in the shins as hard as she could.

"Fuck!" It came out quietly, and he glared at her. "Do that again and you'll be sorry. And keep quiet, we're both dead if we're caught."

Dead was better than captured. Carise opened her mouth to scream, but Fynn anticipated it and stuck something on her face. It stuck like a horrible mass of spiderwebs and crawled over her tongue, muting her.

He grinned evilly at her and pulled her forward.

They moved slower now, and Carise could see weapons mounted on the top of the building, slowly swerving from right to left. She didn't see soldiers anywhere near them and wondered if it was some kind of artificial intelligence that powered them. Maybe it was drawn to sound.

Maybe that was why no enemy soldiers were sneaking in through that entrance.

She couldn't be sure. With the substance on her mouth she couldn't ask, and she couldn't trust that Fynn would tell her the truth. Kidnappers weren't notorious for being honest.

They seemed to cross some invisible line and she could see Fynn relax. He started to move faster and tugged harder on her arm. Carise didn't want to move, but she feared what he'd do to her if she refused. She knew the tortures a kidnapper could inflict on his captive.

Why? She wanted to demand. Fynn had seemed nice to her before. Sure, he was flirtatious, but she didn't think he was consumed by lust and the need to own her. She got the idea that Fynn wasn't a one woman kind of alien.

The streets were strangely deserted, the fighting on the other side of the palace. It was almost possible to pretend that it wasn't happening at all.

Would anyone come to help Mad if things took a turn

for the worse? Or would the city turn against him, happy to devour his corpse?

"Ah, here we are," said Fynn, finally coming to a stop in a darkened, narrow alleyway between two stone buildings.

Three men materialized out of the shadows and Carise didn't recognize them. The one in the center was clearly the leader. He looked Carise up and down like he owned her and grinned in a way that made her stomach roil.

"So you're not completely useless," the man said to Fynn.

The central man stepped into a small pool of light, and Carise got a better look and felt even more sick. No, she did recognize this man. She'd seen him pull a human on a leash. And he'd kidnapped her once before.

Baryn.

Baryn stepped forward and placed a finger under her chin, tilting her head up and then moving it from side to side. He scowled at the substance over her mouth. "Remove this," he commanded Fynn.

Fynn shrugged. "It will dissolve with a bit of water. Spit might even do it. It's not meant to be permanent."

Carise did her best to lick at the substance, trying to dissolve it from within, but it tasted horrible and she gagged. Still, she kept it up. Better not to be muzzled.

Baryn reached a hand back, and one of his men produced a small flask. He uncorked it and splashed water on her face. Carise flinched at the cold. But already she could feel the substance starting to slip off her skin.

"That's better," said Baryn. "I've got a use for her mouth."

She tried to struggle, tried to run, but there were too many men around her and she couldn't do much.

"Don't worry." Baryn unclipped a length of leather from his belt and wrapped it around her wrists. "It'll be fun for both of us." His fingers trailed up her arms and made her shiver in fright. "All that energy flowing through you. And it will all be for me. You're better than a Pitcher."

It made no sense at first. Then she remembered her conversation with Jaek. Pitchers were some kind of energy source that came from the Fount on Krudare. And Kru'dari could suck energy out of humans.

She didn't want to be Baryn's battery.

She lunged at him with no hope of victory. Her only chance of escape now was death, and she'd rather have that than be used by this terrible man.

But Baryn got hold of her and her struggles were useless.

"Is our business concluded?" Fynn asked, sounding as bored as any man could after concluding a hostage exchange. "You stop coming for the bounty and leave me alone. Yes?"

Baryn stared at Fynn for several seconds before giving a single nod. "Stay out of our way and we won't trouble you."

That didn't sound like the kind of promise that Fynn was looking for, but Carise couldn't find it in herself to feel bad for him. He'd screwed her over, now he was getting screwed.

"That's not what we agreed," Fynn insisted. "Guerran's a small planet."

One of Baryn's men pulled a knife, and it glinted in the small pool of light. "It's the best deal you'll get," said Baryn. "Now be on your way before I change my mind."

Fynn spat at Baryn's feet, but danced out of the way before any harm could be done to him. And then he melted into the night, nothing more than a shadow.

Carise hoped someone stabbed him.

"Come with me, little girl." Baryn tugged her deeper into the alley.

Carise's mind went blank, and when she could think again, all she could do was scream.

Jaek!

26

JAEK FLINCHED at the pounding in his head. He'd had headaches before. Who didn't? But this one had come out of nowhere and threatened to pound a hole in his skull. Not an opportune time in the middle of battle.

"What are they doing?" Mad asked as they surveyed the enemy across the no man's land of the street between them.

The fighting wasn't over, but it had calmed down to little more than a brawl. And Jaek didn't like it. The first volleys of aerial bombardment from Mad's side had cowed the enemy. For a few moments. But they had catapults of their own, and the stones they were chucking at them could take down the palace walls if they hit it right.

He needed to check on Carise.

The instinct had been battering him for the last half hour and Jaek had almost fled the battlefield to look for her. It was only the smell of blood in the air and the sounds of soldiers dying that kept him rooted in place. He was needed here. She was safe inside.

Or she should have been.

But everything in his soul told him to find her and make sure.

Jaek! Her voice echoed in his head, and he stumbled.

He didn't think twice before his heart sent out the binding link of the mate bond. It wasn't a choice. It was necessity. And when it clicked into place almost immediately, Jaek's stomach roiled with certainty.

"Carise is in danger." The words were out of his mouth before he chose to speak. Mad snapped a look at him, eyebrows raised.

He had to find her. He needed her. He loved her. And he had to protect her. The mate bond wasn't psychic, not really, but mates could feel a general sense of one another. And what he was feeling from Carise right now was far from good.

Fear. Anger. Dread.

It could be the battle, but he knew it was more.

And before he could tell Mad he was going to find Carise, the fighting around them died down to near silence as their enemy retreated.

Had they won? Was surrender imminent?

"I demand the exile king!" yelled a harsh voice from the center of the enemy contingent. He yelled it over and over until his men started stamping their feet and beating their shields in a pounding rhythm.

No, the battle wasn't over yet.

A column opened in their line and Mad walked through it, Kenzie and Jaek flanking him. Jaek wasn't surprised to see Baryn standing there, clad in battle leathers and holding a knife.

But that knife was held to Carise's throat. Her eyebrow was cut and her cheek looked swollen, as if she'd been slapped or punched. She scowled and spat, and he was sure she would have fought back if the knife wasn't there.

Beside him, Kenzie lunged forward, and both Mad and Jaek had to clamp hands down on her shoulders to hold her back. Anger was so strong in Jaek he couldn't say a word. The primal urge to scream until his throat bled was all that was left.

"I'm here," Mad said as the commotion around them died down. "Stop this madness, Baryn. Leave my territory and I won't kill you."

A noise escaped Jaek, and he had to strain every muscle to keep from killing Baryn for Mad. He'd just let him *go?* While the exile held Carise captive?

Jaek could feel her fear, her panic, and a strange sense of calm. Their eyes met for a moment and Jaek could breathe.

Mad might let Baryn live. Jaek made no promises.

Baryn grinned with all of the malice that lived in him and handed Carise over to another of his lieutenants who also held a knife on her, though not as closely as Baryn had. "I challenge you, Mad Damari. I'm going to be the exile king by morning, and you'll be nothing but meat."

What game was Baryn playing at? He was a decent fighter, but not one that should be so confident. Kenzie had once beaten him in the fighting pits, though she'd spared his life that night.

A mistake they were all now paying for.

"What do you say, Mad?" Baryn prompted when the silence stretched.

Jaek reached out and squeezed Mad's arm to get his attention. His best friend gave him a look and then nodded in understanding. Mad turned back to Baryn. "I accept. Jaek shall act as my champion."

Kenzie made a frustrated noise, no doubt wanting to rush into the ring herself, but she didn't try and stop the fight.

Baryn smiled again. "When he's dead, my first move will be to execute you. As for your queen?" Baryn's eyes flicked up and down, taking in Kenzie. "Perhaps I'll keep her around. Sisters reunited at last."

"I will slice your balls off and make you eat them before you lay a finger on me," Kenzie spat.

"Passion." Baryn's eyes got bright, and he seemed to enjoy the threat.

"Let's do this." Jaek was done grandstanding. "Set up the ring."

There weren't any official rules for a challenge, though there were customs. And Baryn seemed to be abiding by them. The soldiers from both camps made a large circle in the street, giving Baryn and Jaek plenty of room to fight in.

Jaek couldn't fail. The only way to protect Carise was to win. And he couldn't let down his mate. Or his best friend, who would lose his position and his life if he failed.

Jaek wasn't a fighter, but he knew the siren song of bloodshed. But today he would fight to win. His fingers tightened around his axe, the weight not quite familiar or welcome, but the edge sharp enough to do the damage he needed.

He stalked into the makeshift ring, only a few feet separating him from Baryn, who looked absolutely gleeful at the prospect of the fight.

He's regret it. If he lived long enough. Jaek didn't care about making him suffer, not today. All he cared about was making him dead.

He couldn't look at Carise. Already crimson rage flowed in his veins, and if he looked at his mate, he'd lose all strategy. He needed to focus. Baryn was no great fighter, though he was accomplished enough. And anyone could get in a lucky shot.

Jaek wouldn't fail.

He found his center and waited. A minute ticked by, and then another.

And then, at the moment the fight began, Jaek charged.

27

Something had changed.

Carise barely worried about the knife that was held a few inches from her throat. She could still feel the scratch from the one that Baryn had held against her, ready to bleed her dry with a flick of his wrist. The few inches of air between her and naked steel right now might have been a mile.

Instead, her mind was preoccupied. She could *feel* Jaek. Not just the emotions that lived in her heart for him. She could feel what he was feeling.

Soulmates are real.

That was what Kenzie said. It was what Carise hoped deep in her heart she was to Jaek. And perhaps there'd been some bond that flourished between them in the last few minutes. She didn't understand it and she couldn't ask anyone about it right now, not when she was surrounded by enemies and watching her love fight for his life.

She wanted to look away as Jaek and Baryn clashed, machete against axe. It was hard to believe that she'd loved action movies back when she lived on Earth. Then she'd been exhilarated by fast cars, sharp knives, and shiny guns.

Seeing it in person made her want to vomit.

But she couldn't look away. She felt like she owed it to Jaek to watch. And she didn't trust Baryn one bit. His voice had been slimy with triumph as he issued the challenge, and she could have sworn that she saw one of his men hand him something that he'd slipped into a discreet pocket before stepping into the ring.

A secret weapon?

Or was her mind playing tricks on her?

She watched intently. Already Baryn had a cut on his cheek from a mean punch from Jaek, but Jaek had been nicked by Baryn's knife. She *knew* Jaek was a better fighter than this, so why was he holding back?

Baryn and Jaek came together in a flash of movement and then retreated. That was all the fight was, clash and retreat, clash and retreat. And in one of those clashes, eventually one of them would land a real blow.

And then it would be over.

It felt like it had been going on forever, but it couldn't have been more than a handful of minutes. *Come on, Jaek.* She wanted to yell her encouragement, but she couldn't risk distracting Jaek.

Or making the exile at her throat remember he was holding a knife.

That was her thought. Until she saw Baryn reach a hand into his pocket and pull out something that glinted in the moonlight before he concealed it in his fist.

Had Jaek seen? What was that?

They circled each other again, and Carise forgot about worry for herself. "There's something in his fist!" she yelled and dodged to the side before she could be stabbed. Still, she braced for some kind of punishment.

It never came.

The Kru'dari beside her slumped to the ground, an arrow piercing the back of his throat. That arrow hadn't come from Mad's people.

Carise looked behind and saw a shadow move on a rooftop, but she couldn't see anything else, and she couldn't look away for long. Strangely, the exiles around her didn't seem to pay attention to their dead fellow. They were too engrossed by the fight.

Whatever trick Baryn had tried to pull, it hadn't worked. There was a shiny bit of metal fallen on the ground near the edge of the fighting and Carise took a chance, scrambling two steps forward and kicking it into the crowd before Baryn could get close to it again.

That the enemy noticed and yanked her back to stand in place.

Jaek and Baryn clashed again, but this time there was a pained male groan and they didn't separate. Jaek swung his axe, and it connected with a meaty thud that made Carise want to throw up.

Jaek tugged on the axe, but it was buried in Baryn's side too deep for him to yank it out. So he let go, and he let the dying man have it with his fists.

Baryn fell completely to the ground and Jaek stood, blood covering him and death in his eyes.

A brief cheer went up around Mad's people, but Carise could feel the mood about to break. It didn't matter what the agreement was before that challenge, the men around her wanted blood.

Another soldier beside her went down with an arrow notched through his throat, and all hell broke loose.

Carise dropped down and snatched up a machete from the fallen man. She didn't know how to use it, but in close quarters it was her only defense. But the soldiers seemed to forget about her.

Most of them, anyway.

They charged at Mad's people, but during the challenge they'd had a chance to regroup, and though she could hear fighting, it sounded far more organized than any brawl.

Two Kru'dari, however, didn't ignore her. They flashed leering smiles and tried to advance on her.

Carise waved the machete. She was no fighter, but she wasn't going to let them take her. That was that.

Before the exiles could get in knife range, Jaek's huge body busted through the crowd and stood between her and the Kru'dari. They stood no chance against her terrifying mate.

And he let his rage out on them.

Perhaps Carise should have been afraid, but she couldn't summon any fear when it came to Jaek, not when she trusted him so completely. Not when he stood between her and those who would do her harm.

She was done running.

Sometime later—it could have been minutes or hours; time had a strange way of flowing in the battle—a horn sounded. It sounded like something a Viking would have used, and it caused a ripple to go through the soldiers around them.

"You are surrounded!" Mad's voice boomed out, amplified. "Put down your weapons or die. Your leader is dead. The challenge has failed. Surrender."

There was a pregnant moment where Carise didn't know how things would go. Would these men fight to the death for a leader who'd already fallen? Or would they do the wise thing and live to fight another day?

They were smarter than Baryn, it turned out.

First one, then another, then a wave of men let their weapons fall and put their hands up. There was some frustrated grumbling that could have come from anyone, but the fighting subsided to nothing.

"Take them inside," the order went out, and columns of guards formed around the enemy soldiers, leading them into the palace for whatever punishment awaited them.

And eventually the crowd thinned down to barely anyone. There were servants and guards tending to the injured and the fallen, and a patrol ringed the street to make sure no one else came for Mad.

Otherwise, it was just her and Jaek.

"Who shot the arrows?" she asked. She and Jaek had drifted somewhat away from the enemy who had held her, but if she looked back, she could still see their bodies. She'd never seen so many dead before. And maybe the horror of it would wash over her eventually, but right now she was just relieved to be alive.

Jaek wiped away some of the blood on his face with his sleeve. He looked up to the roof opposite them. "I saw movement, but there's no way that was one of Mad's men. I'm sure he'll look into it. Come on." He nodded toward the palace, but didn't touch her. "Let's go inside."

There were three feet of space between them, and Jaek wasn't eager to close that distance. Carise did it herself, grabbing his hand, heedless of the fact it was covered in blood.

Jaek tried to pull away, but she tightened her grip.

"You shouldn't have to see me like this," he said, face angled away from her.

Carise stepped around him so he couldn't hide. Not that a seven-foot-tall warrior could actually hide on an open street. "As what? My protector? My champion?"

"There's no honor in this."

"My mate?" The words rang out, louder than they should have been. Carise stepped even closer to Jaek and reached up to run her fingers across his cheek. "That's what this is, isn't it?" She raised their joined hands to rest on her heart. "Do you feel it too?"

"You called. I answered." He swallowed hard, but was still holding himself back. "You deserve more than this."

He was right. They needed off this battlefield. But it wasn't Carise's nerves that needed to be tended. She wanted to kiss him right there. To tell him again that she loved him and wanted him. But with the echoes of battle all around them, Jaek couldn't see it.

He could fight, but he had a gentle soul. He didn't need to see all of this destruction.

She stepped back just enough and led him into the palace.

28

Jaek knew he should let Carise go. He'd unleashed the darkest parts of himself and she'd been forced to watch as he killed and killed and killed. All to keep her safe. How could she see him as anything but a monster?

And yet he felt as docile as a lamb as she led him through the halls of the palace to his rooms. She pushed him inside and then opened the door to the shower room, letting the water run until the steam started to escape into the bedroom.

Carise looked up at him with love in her eyes, and Jaek had to look away before the emotion swallowed him. Soon she would realize what he was, what he'd done, and she'd turn away.

She would have to. She was too gentle for Guerran. And if tonight hadn't proved that, some other night soon would.

Carise reached forward and unstrapped his leather

breastplate, carefully setting it on the ground. He'd left his axe buried back in Baryn's body, and he'd sheathed his knife and left it in the bedroom before approaching the shower.

Next his mate carefully untucked his shirt and pushed it up towards his head, but he was so tall, he had to pull it off. Blood stained the fabric, and it would probably need to be burned. Even if the stains came out, Jaek wasn't sure he'd ever be able to wear it again without the memories of tonight haunting him.

"Shoes," Carise said quietly, dropping to her knees to loosen his boots and guide him out of them.

Despite the shame and darkness roiling through him, Jaek's body responded to the sight of his mate on her knees before him. But he did his best to push those thoughts away. How could she want him now?

He wouldn't dare touch her again.

She stood and reached for his pants, undoing the tie and letting them slide down until he was completely naked in front of her. But her eyes stayed glued to his face, and something in Jaek cracked at that.

He squeezed his own eyes shut, as if he could push out the emotions that were trying to crowd in.

And while his eyes were closed, he heard more fabric hit the ground. His eyes snapped open and Carise stood before him naked, her dress pooled on the ground beside his dirty battle clothes.

"In the shower," she told him with a nod to the steamy stream.

Jaek was helpless to resist her, as if he ever could. But no, from the first moment he saw her, he belonged totally to her.

And as he stepped under the water, he started to feel those parts again, the way his broken soul was inexorably bound to hers. Nothing could make him walk away, even if he was braced for the moment Carise would leave him.

Instead, he felt her soapy hands glide over his back, and her words wrapped around his heart. "I was terrified when I was out there," she admitted. "But I knew that as long as I could find you, you'd protect me. That's what you do, Jaek. And not just for me. For everyone you love. Whatever you think you became out there, you're wrong. You fought because you had to. And you're exactly what I need."

Jaek let her wash him, even kneeling down a little to let her get her fingers through his hair. And as she washed him, the shame and doubt melted away, cleaned by his mate as if it was only dirt.

"Whatever you want, I am yours." The confession came out easily, far more so than Jaek would have expected, considering where his thoughts had been only moments before. "If you want to leave Guerran, we'll go. If you want…"

She spun him around and looked up at him, a strange smile on her face. Water cascaded over his shoulders like he was standing in a rain storm, but he ignored it. "No big decisions while we're washing the battle off."

He looked down at his arms and then back at his mate. "I'm all clean now."

Her grin turned heated. "So you are. Planning to do anything about that?"

She was right, thoughts of the future could wait. Jaek stepped into her space until she backed up, feet hitting the small bench that lined the back of the shower. He leaned down and captured her lips with his own, the kiss searing deep down into his soul.

Yes. This he could do forever.

But as he shifted, his foot slipped, and he would have gone flying if he didn't brace himself against the wall in time. He and Carise broke apart and stared at one another, laughter glinting in each of their eyes.

He reached over and flicked off the stream of water, and then handed his mate a towel before quickly toweling himself off as well. He would have gladly taken her while the hot water flowed over them, but not if it would end with one or both of them with heads cracked on the tile.

After quickly drying off, Jaek let the towel drop to the floor and picked up Carise, laughing with her as she made a startled sound. Then he was rushing them into the room where the big bed waited for them.

Was it only this afternoon that he'd been with her here? Time had a funny way of flowing sometimes. He was sure he'd lived several lifetimes in the past few hours.

But once he had Carise laid out on the bed, he forgot

all about time, all about the outside world. His mate lay before him, a sultry look on her face and an invitation in her eyes.

And Jaek knew he had only one purpose: to bring this woman pleasure. She'd unlocked something within him he hadn't known was there, and he felt free for the first, the only, time in his life.

How had he lived before she'd come to him?

He hadn't.

He loomed over her, catching her mouth with his own and capturing her moan as he wedged his leg between her thighs. He loved her little sighs, the way she gave herself over to him with the perfect trust of a mate, and he wanted those sounds imprinted on him forever.

Jaek took his time now, finally believing that he and Carise had their forever. He would protect her from the harms that came their way. He would hold her heart beside his own. And they would build their life together, however they wanted it to look.

He made these promises to himself as he fit himself inside of her, inch by careful inch, watching her eyes widen and darken in pleasure as he filled her. It was its own kind of torture to take things this slowly. The need to thrust as quickly as he could, to make it hard and fast and pounding threatened to take him over.

But not today. Today he worshiped his mate. He cared for her. Just as she'd cared for him.

And as she cried out, her body rippling around him, Jaek let himself get swept up in the heat of it, his own body finding its release as he held onto her and promised to never let go.

He whispered words of love into the bend of her neck, and from the tiny sounds of assent she made, he knew she heard them. But this wouldn't be the only time. He'd tell her every day, and show her even more.

"Mate," Jaek sighed against her, as their bodies gave up to the exhaustion of the previous day and they both began to slowly lose the battle to sleep.

But not before Carise whispered back. "Mate."

29

Leaving their room that morning was hard. Really hard. Especially with Jaek giving her heated looks and lying in bed like some sex god. But there would be time for that later.

Carise had something she had to do this morning.

She was glad to find Kenzie alone in a small training area. She watched for a few moments as Kenzie worked out frustration on a wooden target, her knives doing the kind of damage that would leave a person dead.

At times like these, Carise didn't recognize her sister. This wasn't the Kenzie who'd left Earth so long ago with stars in her eyes and a fancy job on a space colony calling her name.

This was a warrior.

But she also knew that Kenzie didn't always recognize the new Carise. They'd each changed far more than they could have predicted over the last two years. And now it was time to make peace with that.

She wanted her sister back.

Kenzie finished her sequence and gave the target one final kick, making the stand almost fall over. Then she sheathed her weapons, grabbed a towel to wipe off her sweat, and turned to look at Carise.

"You look well rested," her sister said, exchanging the towel for a glass of water and sipping.

Carise couldn't help her blush and hoped that Kenzie didn't notice. "I slept well," was what she settled on. It was true, after all.

Awkward silence stretched between them, and Carise didn't know how to break it. Maybe she shouldn't have come here after all. Or at least she should have come with a plan.

She remembered now that it wasn't always easy to talk to her sister. Life on Earth had been filled with its own awkward silences and misunderstandings. And that was comforting in its own way.

Maybe they could have that again.

Eventually.

"I'm sorry," Kenzie said.

It caught Carise by surprise, but she kept her mouth shut and let her sister talk.

"I'm sorry I slipped you that melatonin. I should have asked, or at least told you. You were completely right to be upset. And I'm sorry I didn't let you get a word in edgewise that night. I was so happy, so relieved, and so *scared* that I wasn't thinking straight. And I fucked up." She sat on a bench and braced her hands on her knees, but she didn't ask for Carise's forgiveness.

Did she think Carise wouldn't give it?

"I'm sorry for running away like I did. I should have stayed and talked." She could still remember the fear that had washed through her when she woke up, the certainty that Kenzie would drag her away from Guerran and Jaek and she'd never see him again.

They were silent for several moments, but it was a little less awkward. A little better.

"You know," Kenzie said eventually, "we've got plenty of room here. You're welcome to stay."

But Carise remembered the giant of a man she'd left back in her bed, and she smiled while she shook her head. "I don't think so."

Kenzie didn't offer to let Jaek move in. Probably for the best. She and Jaek didn't seem to like each other too well. Carise hoped it improved. She didn't want any future get togethers to be awkward.

Was there something like Thanksgiving on Guerran? Now *that* would be awkward.

"So you and Jaek."

Carise nodded. "Me and Jaek. You and Mad. I don't think we've done too bad for ourselves."

And Kenzie smiled in a way Carise had never seen before. She didn't know her sister could look so... sweet. Wow. Guerran really did have a way of changing people.

Or maybe that was love.

"Lunch," Kenzie said suddenly.

"What?" It was still morning and Carise was still full from breakfast.

"Let's do lunch every week." Kenzie shook her head and held up a hand. "I'm sorry. I mean, how do you feel about doing lunch once a week? Or some other get together? I'd like to see you more often."

"I'd like that too." They set up a tentative meeting, and Carise gave Kenzie a long hug, finally feeling happy that she and her sister were back together all these years. "We're going to be okay," she said before finally turning away.

Kenzie nodded. "Yeah, I think we are."

They didn't spend much more time together. Apparently being Mad's exile queen came with duties of its own, and Kenzie took her job seriously. She offered to let Carise tag along, but there was somewhere else Carise needed to be.

She found Jaek in the hallway outside of their room, his hand pushing the door open. "Did you steal the crown jewels?" she teased. He had a cloth sack in his other hand and it was half hidden behind his back.

"What?" Jaek blinked and then looked down at his bounty. He gave a small laugh. "The only raid was to the kitchens. Mad's palace is better stocked than our place."

"Our?" Presumption from Kenzie made Carise want to pull her hair out, but that one word from Jaek had her dancing with giddiness. "Our place?"

Jaek's eyes got wide, and he seemed to recognize that

he'd slipped up. But he recovered quickly. "My home is yours. If you want it. I want you in my life and in my bed. Our bed. You're my mate, Carise, and I love you. Come home with me?"

Her seven-foot-tall alien hunk looked a bit worried. As if she would say no. She stepped in close, got on her tip toes, and waited patiently for him to bend down enough so she could give him the kiss she so richly deserved.

"Of course I'm coming home with you, Jaek. It's where we belong." She pulled him inside of their temporary quarters. "But while we're here..." She nodded towards the bed and gave Jaek a wicked grin.

He scooped her up and strode to the bed, and Carise let out a whoop of joy.

Yes. As long as they were together, that was where they belonged.

EPILOGUE

Fynn hadn't slept, and his stomach was tied in knots from two days without eating. If Baryn wasn't already dead, he would hunt him down himself. Damn the bastard.

Bile curdled in Fynn's stomach, but there was nothing left to vomit up.

He'd done more than his fair share of terrible things in his life, but what he'd done to the cute human was a step farther than he ever thought he'd go. It was one thing to betray a bad person to save his own hide, but an innocent one?

He was a monster.

But he was a monster who'd survived another day.

Fynn broke down his simple bow and threw the wood into the fire that raged in the fire pit. It wouldn't do to be caught with that thing, not that it was, in and of itself, incriminating. Plenty of exiles carried bows and arrows.

But he didn't need more questions.

There were pieces in motion, things he'd been working at for weeks. All before his carefully constructed existence fell to pieces.

At least he'd had one last favor to call in. And it was the one that might see him survive until his next birthday.

He heard footsteps near his door and then the whisper of a slide of something on the ground. Fynn got up from where he was sitting on the floor and scurried over to find an envelope on the ground. Whoever had delivered it was already gone.

That was for the best. Look what he'd done to the last courier.

He pulled out the notecard and read the message.

Green Zone shipyard. End of week. Silver Waves.

A location, a date, and a ship. If Fynn was quick enough, he'd find his way off this terrible planet and snatch something like freedom from the jaws of death.

Of course, his picture was plastered up on wanted posters all over the Green Zone, from another one of his stunning betrayals.

Getting to the Silver Waves would be a suicide run. He looked into the fire and smiled.

At least it would be fun.

———

Thank you for reading *Exile's Adored*!
I'd appreciate it so much if you would consider leaving a review.

The series will continue!

WHAT'S TO READ NEXT: SYNNR'S SAINT

Taken from Earth and used like a lab rat...

Emily was a normal law student until she was abducted by aliens. Forced to perform death defying feats by night and undergoing medical tests by day, she doesn't know how much longer she can take it. When one alien takes particular interest in her she's afraid things have gone from bad to worse. He's got wings and fangs, and he makes her heart pound. But she can't want an alien like that... can she?

He doesn't have time to rescue a human...

Oz is on Kilrym for a reason, and it's not to rescue the ethereal performer who captivates him by night. But covert ops are impossible when his mind is on the human who could be his fated mate. War is on the horizon, but what if the only way to save his people is to sacrifice Emily?

Despite the fact that they were born light years apart, they are a perfect match. But Oz is keeping secrets, and when Emily finds out the truth she may never be able to forgive him, no matter how much she needs him to survive and escape the planet alive.

ALSO BY KATE RUDOLPH

Looking for something else? Kate Rudolph has a heart pounding collection or paranormal and sci-fi romance stories for you! Bundles, bears, audiobooks, aliens, and more. Check out your options in the list below. You can find out all you need to know at www.katerudolph.net.

Want to check out one of the books? Click on the series name to find out more!

Dragon Brides

Fated mates, fierce women, and dragon princes.

Crux

Ranger

Saber

———

Alien Mates: Planet Exile

Guerran is no place for pretty human women. But these alien heroes will protect their mates!

Also available in audio!

Exile's Hunter

Exile's Adored

Exile's Escape

———

Zulir Warrior Mates

Kidnapped humans. Alien Warriors. Electric wings.

The Zulir Warrior Mates series brings you human heroines
and heroes abducted from Earth who find love – and wings! –
with the alien warriors who rescue them.

Also available in audio!

Synnr's Saint

Synnr's Hope

Synnr's Spark

Synnr's Kiss

———

Guarded by the Shifter

Werewolf. Bodyguard. Mate.

The origins of these shifters are shrouded in mystery, but
they're determined to protect their mates from any harm that
comes their way.

Also available in audio!

Hunting Season

On the Prowl

Stalking Magic

Detyen Warriors

Detya was destroyed a hundred years ago. These doomed warriors are out to find justice... and their mates.

The Detyen Warriors series brings you kick butt heroines, alpha alien heroes, fated mates, and relationships strong enough to span the galaxy!

The entire series is also available in audio!

Soulless

Ruthless

Heartless

Faultless

Endless

Alien Holiday Romance

Christmas... in space????

These alien holiday romances look beyond Earth's winter

holidays and ring in the season across the galaxy! ***Select titles available in audio.***

Snowed in with the Alien Beast

The Alien's Winter Gift

The Alien Reindeer's Wild Ride

Trapped with her Alien Mate

Alien Outlaws

Outlaws, schemes, and love… it's all there in the Alien Outlaws series…

Andie Munster is sick of life on Ixilta, the planet she got dumped on after being abducted from Earth six years ago. And when the mysterious and dangerous Xandr shows up looking for a way off the planet, she's half-prisoner, half-co-conspirator in a wild rush to escape.

Rogue Alien's Escape

Rogue Alien's Woman

Rogue Alien's Secret

Rogue Alien's Legacy

Mated to the Alien

Fated Mate Alien Romance

Detyens are doomed to die young if they don't find their fated mates.

Follow along as these mated pairs fight off aliens, corrupt dictators, prejudiced humans, pirates, and more! The books can be read or listened to in any order, though some characters show up in multiple stories.

Select books available in audio.

Pick a book and jump into the action today!

Ruwen

Tyral

Stoan

Cyborg

Krayter

Kayleb

Shayn

Braxtyn

Doryan

Dekon

———

Stealing the Alpha

The thief takes what she wants, but the alpha keeps what's his...

Join shifter thief Mel as she clashes with lion alpha Luke in an explosive trilogy of two opposites who can't keep away from one another.

Also available in audio!

The Alpha Heist

Entangled with the Thief

In the Alpha's Bed

Save with box sets!

Aliens. Shifters. Warriors. Mates. Get them all wrapped together in these special box sets. Save up to 30% off the price of buying the individual books, depending on the series!

Alien Outlaws: The Complete Series

Mated to the Alien Volume One (also available in audio)

Mated to the Alien Volume Two (also available in audio)

Mated to the Alien Volume Three

Mated to the Alien Volume Four

Stealing the Alpha: The Complete Series (also available in audio)

The Mate Bundle

Detyen Warriors Volume One (also available in audio)

Detyen Warriors Volume Two (also available in audio)

Zulir Warrior Mates Volume One (also available in audio)

Standalone Paranormal and Sci-Fi Romance:

Crashed

Mated on the Moon

Mated to the Alien Dragon

Marked

Bear in Mind

Alpha's Mercy

Gemma's Mate

Find more by Kate Rudolph at www.katerudolph.net

ABOUT KATE RUDOLPH

Kate Rudolph is a paranormal and alien romance author who lives in Indiana. She loves writing about kick butt heroines and the steamy heroes who love them. She's been devouring romance novels since she was too young to be reading them and had to hide her books so no one would take them away. She couldn't imagine a better job in this world than writing romances and sharing them with her fellow readers.

If you enjoyed this story, please consider leaving a review.